EYE of the MOON

DIANNE HOFMEYR

EYE of the MOON

Aladdin

NEW YORK   LONDON   TORONTO   SYDNEY

ALADDIN

An imprint of Simon & Schuster Children's Publishing Division
1230 Avenue of the Americas, New York, NY 10020
First Aladdin paperback edition June 2011
Copyright © 2007 by Dianne Hofmeyr
Originally published in Great Britain in 2007 by Simon & Schuster UK Ltd, a CBS company.
Published by arrangement with Simon & Schuster UK Ltd.
All rights reserved, including the right of reproduction in whole or in part in any form.
ALADDIN is a trademark of Simon & Schuster, Inc.,
and related logo is a registered trademark of Simon & Schuster, Inc.
For information about special discounts for bulk purchases, please contact Simon & Schuster
Special Sales at 1-866-506-1949 or business@simonandschuster.com.
The Simon & Schuster Speakers Bureau can bring authors to your live event.
For more information or to book an event contact the Simon & Schuster Speakers Bureau
at 1-866-248-3049 or visit our website at www.simonspeakers.com.
Designed by Ann Zeak and Irene Metaxatos
The text of this book was set in Centaur MT.
Manufactured in the United States of America 0511 OFF
2 4 6 8 10 9 7 5 3 1
Library of Congress Control Number 2010940169
ISBN 978-1-4424-1188-3
ISBN 978-1-4424-1189-0 (eBook)

For David

MOON

Ruler of the Stars.
Protector of Women.
Eye of Wisdom, Truth,
and Secrets.

✦ ✕ ✦ ✕ ✦ ✕ ✦ ✕ ✦

With two fingers missing it's hard to grip a reed stylus. So I'm writing with difficulty as I sit here on the bank of the Great River far from the city of Thebes. At last it's quiet. The noise of battle has ended. Only the lapping of the water through the reeds keeps me company.

I hope my story will soon be carved in stone so the truth will be known to all. I've a great many things to tell. Poison, slavery, and murder are all part of it. If it seems too much like myth, let me swear the words are written by the white feather of Truth, under the protection of the Eye of the Moon.

When all is told, I will add:

These are the words of Isikara—daughter of the embalmer at the temple of the crocodile god, Sobek.

But first I should explain my injury.

The forefinger and the middle finger are the bow fingers. They pluck the gut and send the arrow with purpose. Strength is crucial in pulling back the bowstring. But it's the final release of these fingers that controls the arrow and sets it on its path.

Right to the heart of the enemy.

I hadn't understood their true importance until my right hand was forced open against the ground, a cleaver raised, and both fingers sliced through with one clean blow.

What better way to maim a bowman than to take away these fingers?

Of the two of us, my friend Anoukhet was the better marksman. She pulled the arrow back with the strength of someone twice her size and sent it on its way with the true eye of a hunter. Deadly accurate!

Side by side we stood. And side by side we were captured. Sisters in combat.

But that's behind us now. I've put aside my arrow and bow and changed my boy's tunic for a robe more suited to a girl. Anoukhet has too. But a girl's robe doesn't prevent her from remaining fiery. And we both still carry daggers in our belts.

It might seem strange that a girl writes of warfare. There are many strange things ahead. Not least that I should be *able* to write. Few girls are scribes. But my father taught me well in the way of writing words in the new hieratic style. It's quicker than hieroglyphics and suits my impatience.

There is much to tell. My words flow fast ahead of me now and my stylus blots the sooty ink and leaves behind dark smudges on the papyrus. The story grows so fast, that should I not be able to find enough soot and sap to mix more ink, I would write it in blood . . . even my own.

✦ ✕ ✦ ✕ ✦ ✕ ✦ ✕ ✦

1

THE GREAT CROCODILE GOD, SOBEK

My story begins in the Temple of Sobek in Thebes on the day I thought my brother would die.

There was a moment of absolute stillness. Then my brother's scream. I can still hear it. The worst scream I've ever heard.

I ran down the path to the crocodile pit. He clung to the edge of the stone wall.

"The stick, Kara! Get the stick!" Katep bellowed.

His eyes were glazed with terror. A crocodile held his arm and was wrenching and tossing its head in a fury. Inside the pit, the other crocodiles were thrashing and snapping in their eagerness to get at my brother as well.

I searched frantically. The forked crocodile stick that usually stood next to the wall wasn't there. Nothing was in its place. I had no weapon. Not even a branch to shove between the beast's jaws or poke at its eyes.

I stood paralyzed. I knew how brutal crocodiles were. One thrust of its tail, one quick arch of its body, and it would throw Katep into the air and then catch him again in a stronger, more *fatal* grip.

"*Do* something, Kara!"

I spun around frantically. Grabbed whatever I could. Sand and more sand. And flung it as hard as I could straight at the eyes of the reptile. Again and again, I sent a hailstorm of sand into the air.

Suddenly, with a wild, angry snort, the crocodile shook its head viciously. Then it lost its grip on my brother and sank back below the wall into the pit. Katep fell limply to the ground at my feet, blood streaming from an arm so torn that it no longer looked like an arm.

There was so much blood. I thought he would die. How could anyone live when there was so much blood everywhere?

But he didn't die.

The crocodiles are kept in a pit at the temple for sacrifice. Katep was responsible for feeding and caring for them. My father makes sacred offerings of them to appease Sobek. At certain times of the moon the crocodiles are ritually washed, and then one is chosen, killed, and embalmed as an offering.

Katep's work is to look after the crocodiles. My work is to help my father with embalming. To mix the resins and prepare the linen mummy wraps. Crocodiles are cumbersome and difficult to wrap. The bindings have to cross over one another and make a woven pattern. Afterward eyes and teeth are painted on the mummy.

That's the part I enjoy most—painting the ferocious eyes and terrible teeth. But I can never manage to make them as frightening in death as they are in real life.

The mummified crocodiles are placed in special sacred vaults below the temple to keep Sobek company. Row upon row of them, they line up on the stone shelves like so many loaves of bread. Food for the gods.

Since Katep's accident, the job of caring for the crocodiles has fallen to me.

Katep's wound has healed to an angry stump, but the healing of his heart has taken longer. He's restless. The accident has left him silent and resentful, with a smoldering anger. You see, Katep is a hunter . . . *was* a hunter. He can . . . *could* bring down any wildfowl with the flick of his throw-stick and stop any hare in midspring with his arrow.

But no more. The loss of an arm is a terrible misfortune, especially for a hunter like Katep. Without being able to hunt, Katep is no longer Katep.

"I'm leaving!" he announces one morning.

"Leaving?"

He shrugs impatiently. "I have no place here. *Everything* I do requires the skill of both hands. I feel trapped. I *have* to go."

I stare back at him. He knows that I know he is looking for the impossible. "Where will you go?"

"I'm not sure."

"So?"

He shrugs again. It seems his shoulders have forgotten there is only one arm to move. "To the camel dealers' camps in the desert. Or to find gold and amethysts in Nubia. Or to the turquoise workings of Sinai."

I eye him. He might as well have said he is leaving this earth and going into the Underworld. "So far?" is all I say.

His silence tells me he knows what I'm really saying: *How will you manage anywhere with only the stump of an arm?*

"I'll never see you again," I blurt out. "Nubia and Sinai are all far beyond Egypt's borders. They're our *enemies!*"

He gives me a fleeting smile. His face is handsome, despite his anger. "Egypt's enemies, not mine, Kara!" Then he shakes his head. "I *can't* stay here. I can't be a priest or even a stonemason as Father wants me to be."

I kick the sand with my bare foot. "Why not?" I ask, even though I understand his determination to leave. I know he *will* go—no matter how much I plead.

He brandishes the stump of his arm. Beats the

air with it. "Have you heard of a stonemason cutting stone with something like this?"

The scars on the stump of his arm are still raw and red. Dreadful to look at. But at the same time fascinating. I know each scar as well as the moles on my own arms. I've cleaned them, smeared the wounds with unguents, and bound them daily, ever since that day I'd had to hold him down while my father injected the arm with scorpion venom to numb it and cut away the shreds of flesh before stitching the skin together.

Now the scars of the wounds make hieroglyphs across his flesh. The hieroglyphs tell their own story.

I know Katep cannot bear to look at them. It's a burden for him to carry this stump around. No wonder he wants to run away. It's not me or Father that he's running from. It's his arm.

I know this in my head but my heart makes me speak out differently.

"Don't go! *Please* don't go! I'm begging you. You can't leave. You said we'd go away *together* one day. We made plans. Remember? In the fork of the mimosa tree the day we watched the crocodiles laying eggs in the sand."

He gives me a look. "We were children then."

I flick the side plaits of my wig back from my face and squint back at him. I feel like a chastised child. "Is that *all* your promise counts for?"

We had pricked our thumbs with mimosa thorns. I had put my thumb hard against his and mingled our blood. It was a sacred vow. There hadn't been a need. Our blood is already bonded. We share the same thoughts. Between us there is a thread as fine and silvery as a spider's web. Invisible but strong. It's difficult to break.

"Half the boat belongs to me!" I snap. But he knows I'm really saying, *Who will catch fish with me now? Or trap and roast frogs? Or dare me to walk along the wall of the crocodile pit?*

He stares back at me. He has read my thoughts. "Promise not to walk on the crocodile wall."

I pull a face at him. "Ha! You never bothered about anything dangerous before! *You* were the one who dared me to enter the tomb labyrinth the first time!"

"That was different. There were two of us. Don't go into the tomb labyrinth alone, Isikara!"

Why is he calling me Isikara instead of Kara? Already I am no longer his sister.

I give him a hot look from between the strands of my hair. "Don't leave me!"

"Then join me."

I shake my head. "By the white feather of Truth, you know I can't! I *can't* break the vow I made our mother on her death pallet. I promised I'd care for Father. Be his temple assistant. Weave the linen. Help boil the resins for embalming. Look after his embalming tools."

I kick the sand again and swallow hard, fighting my tears with anger. "Now I have to look after the crocodiles as well!"

"Don't trust them even if they seem asleep."

"I don't need your advice!" I squint through the sunlight at him, daring him to change his mind.

"Kara, don't be so cross."

Good. He has called me Kara. I'm his sister again.

For a moment he forgets his own anger and grabs me around the neck with his good arm. I sense the other arm wanting to hug me as well. But the stump waves about without direction. He puts on a deep, fierce voice. "Be careful! I am Sobek! I seize like a beast!"

"Stop it! Don't mock Sobek!" I push him away.

My hand flies to the moonstone amulet at my neck. Quickly I draw the Eye of Horus in the sand with my big toe to ward off the evil eye and keep Katep protected.

On the morning he sails, I hand him a small linen bag to hang around his neck. Inside are the bodies of a dried lizard and a frog, as well as a lock of our mother's hair, to keep him safe. I give him a sack of pomegranates and some shelled beans and two loaves with some potted meat of wildfowl. I'd killed the bird myself with my throw-stick to prove that I could manage without my brother.

I hold out a small amulet of blue glass that I'd bartered for at the market. "It's the scorpion goddess, Seqet—to help ward off evil. Watch out for scorpions under the rocks of Sinai."

He laughs. "In Sinai, men are specially employed as scorpion charmers."

Something jabs at my heart as sharp as a scorpion's sting. He hasn't left yet, but already he knows things I don't know. I eye him. "What if their charms don't work?"

"Stop worrying! The scorpion goddess, Seqet, will protect me."

"Then remember to touch her stone." I thrust the blue amulet at him.

He sails down the silver ribbon of water that joins the Great River. I race along the mud bank trying to keep up with his boat. I will that the burden of my running might drag him back like an anchor to the shore. But no . . . his boat travels lightly forward and my feet remain stuck to the bank.

"I'll never see you again!" I call after him, and murmur a quick silent prayer to Hathor to beg that it won't be true.

"Of course you will."

I call out instructions. Anything to hold him back. "Send me signs that you are safe. Say incantations to keep the crocodiles and hippopotamuses away from the boat. Have you remembered your spear and your throw-stick?"

To all this he nods and smiles back at me.

"And beware of crocodiles. If the boat lodges in reeds, don't climb out into the water. Even if it is only up to your ankles!"

He laughs. "Must I remain in the boat for the rest of my life?"

"Just be careful, Katep!"

"Don't worry, I won't be caught again. I've given Sobek my arm as an offering." He grins. Then he tucks the sail rope under his chin so he can raise his left arm in a salute. He gives me his last look. Then he turns his back and begins paddling with his one good arm.

When I can't keep up with him any longer, I stand and watch his reed boat beat against the wind and the choppy waves. I touch the smooth, cool moonstone of Hathor once more and feel for the knots on my plaited reed bracelet. I call upon all that is evil to remain tied up and out of his reach.

I watch his back and the sail grow smaller and smaller until they are nothing but a moth skimming across the water to an unknown place. I blink and narrow my eyes against the breeze to prevent moisture from being squeezed out of them. A lump rises up in my throat like a bloated, angry toad.

With that sail goes my heart. I never thought Katep would take the boat and leave without me. I stare after him and wish with all my heart that my own life will change. But wishing is dangerous. Wishes have a way of coming back to you.

It's said that those who sail the Great River either

look forward or look back. That morning when Katep left, he didn't look back. He stood stiff-backed to the world he had left behind. I'd stared after him, willing him to turn around.

But he didn't! Not once!

The next morning I dragged a slaughtered goat by its horns to the crocodile pit and cursed Katep for leaving me to do his work.

It was a she-goat. I could see by the swollen udder. The goat's kid would be searching among the other goats now, nosing for the full udder of its mother. But my father believed in sacrificing only she-goats to the crocodiles. Male goats were too precious, he said. They carried the seed of the future herd.

What about she-goats? Weren't they the true future of the herd? But my father was impatient with me. Katep's leaving made him more impatient than usual.

The goat was limp and heavy. My father had slit her throat. Flies were already buzzing around the gash. The track left in the sand by her dragging hooves was spattered with drops of blood that glistened like garnets.

I was glad she was already dead. Offerings are usually made alive. But I had begged my father to kill the goat first so I wouldn't have to listen to her bleating.

The nearer I got to the pit, the tighter I clutched the forked stick.

The crocodiles were moving restlessly. They could sense the scent of the she-goat's blood and the warm, sweet smell of her milk. There were the sounds of jaws snapping and angry hisses as they lashed at one another.

"Be careful of their tails!" Katep had warned.

I didn't need his reminder.

My father had been distraught the morning he'd discovered Katep's empty bed. "Why did he leave without bidding farewell? There was no need for him to go. He could have learned the art of embalming from me."

I gave my father a dark look. "Am I not your helper? Is my work not good enough? Katep was never interested in learning to embalm. Besides, it's not his fault he had to leave. It's the fault of a crocodile!"

"Hush! Hold your tongue! To be eaten by the

most sacred crocodile, Sobek, is the greatest honor."

"I'd rather die without honor."

He shook his head. "Kara! Kara! You're too headstrong. It'll get you into trouble yet. You need a mother to groom you in the ways of women. You must learn to think before you speak."

"But——!"

"Enough!"

I understood my father's anger and hurt. We both missed Katep more than we could say. The house was quieter with him gone. Our meals were taken in silence opposite his empty place. The day Katep left, my father inscribed these words above the arch that led to the crocodile pit:

To be devoured by the crocodile god, Sobek, is to be possessed forever by divinity.

Now, as I passed under those words, shivery bumps came up on my arms. They weren't a comfort. I had no desire to be eaten by a crocodile.

I stood ready to heave the goat into the pit when I suddenly realized that when Katep had left, he'd snapped the thread between us—the thread that I thought could never be broken.

2

DAZZLING ATEN

I woke before the water of the Great River stole blue from the sky. Out on the roof terrace, the stars were turning pale in the east. The chilly air brought goose bumps to my arms. I touched the moonstone of the amulet at my throat—three times for good luck—then felt for the seven knots tied in my plaited papyrus bangle and whispered the prayers that would invoke each knot to tie up any evil that might be lurking and keep Katep safe.

My hands moved from amulet to knots without thinking. They were rituals done as easily as breathing or brushing a fly from my face.

The embers in the clay oven were still warm enough to stir into life. I lay down two loaves that had been proving overnight and dragged the embers around them. Soon the smell of warm barley dough rose up into the air.

Then I crept downstairs past my father's sleeping chamber and past Katep's empty corner and stepped outside into the courtyard. It was shadowy and silent. Even the fish in the reflecting pool still slept. The air was heavy with the perfume of figs and ripening dates. I slipped two figs into my girdle bag and then began sweeping the entrance to the courtyard with a mimosa branch to ward off plagues from entering our home that day.

I took two leather buckets and strode down to the river to fetch my father's bathing water. The water buffalo were moving restlessly in their byre, pushing and nosing one another in their eagerness to get at the fresh clumps of sedge. Their horns stood out like dark lyres against the pale sky.

Some mornings a warm desert wind played music

on those lyres. A strange, enchanting song that came from a far-distant place. A sound that made my feet want to dance and swirl away over the sand dunes. Today there was no wind. Just an early chill that made the skin of the buckets stiff as I carried them down to the river's edge.

The floods were coming. I could tell. Every day the water was pushing higher and higher and the small islands were disappearing. Thoth, the god of wisdom and truth, was weighing sunshine and darkness. Soon the day would come when they would balance equally on the scales. And then sunshine would tip heavier.

Each morning as the light crept in from the east, I searched for the tiny sliver of the First Moon. Now this morning it was there—floating just above the edge of the earth. A transparent shaving, as fine as a single thread of spun flax. Finer than a nail paring. I touched the moonstone amulet and invoked Hathor, goddess of the moon, helper of women, to protect me.

The First Moon marked the day of Ritual. And this would be my first Ritual without Katep. The crocodiles would have to be brought down to the stone pool in the river to be cleansed of evil. My father would select one as a sacrifice to Sobek. Then I'd have to prevent it from returning along the passageway that led back to the pit.

The water was smooth, silent, and cold around my ankles. I searched for the telltale signs of bubbles rising up to make sure no wild river crocodile was lurking below the surface. Then I waded in and checked the stone wall of the pool for gaps. It was a bad omen to allow a sacred crocodile to escape.

It was still too early to slide back the stone that opened the passageway. The crocodiles in the pit wouldn't stir themselves until they'd been warmed by the sun. I'd purposely not fed them since giving them the she-goat. Getting them down to the water would be easy. Getting them back to the pit would be difficult. The village children would have to bang cymbals and beat sticks against the walls to urge them on.

"Remember . . . leave a slaughtered goat in the pit," Katep had instructed. "One that's just beginning to rot. The smell of rotting meat brings them out of the water, like flies to a dung heap!"

Now the sweet perfume of lotus lilies drifted across the water. The warmth of the rising sun was drawing up their buds from beneath the water. I watched as their blue petals began opening to reveal brilliant golden hearts. Each evening the lilies closed again and sank back into the dark water, trapping the scent of the golden hearts between their petals again.

This morning I was first at the river. None of the other village girls had arrived. There was a legend that whoever was early enough would be greeted by the most handsome god of all. He was Nefertem, god of the blue lotus and god of the sunrise, who brought the sun into the sky. It was said he'd rise from the river with a lotus on his head and carry the girl away.

But no god appeared this morning, and even if he had, I'm not sure I'd have gone with him.

I filled my buckets and picked some lilies to perfume my father's bathing water, then squeezed the water from the edge of my wrap and turned to walk back. There was a smell of wood smoke. I could hear babies crying and dogs yapping and squabbling over bones at the rubbish heaps. Women coming toward me were singing as they walked to the fields.

Suddenly they were pointing toward the river. "Look! Look!"

My breath caught as I turned.

A huge boat was floating silently across the water. It wasn't the usual barge that collected tithes for the temple granaries—the one that came piled with sacks of grain for my father to store so he could feed the villagers in times of need. Nor was it the barge that brought jars of oil or bolts of linen for the temple storerooms.

This boat seemed to have risen straight from the depths of the river, like some strange exotic water lily, unfurling as the warmth of the sun touched it—its hull carved and patterned in brilliant carnelian, turquoise, and blue, its gold embellishments dazzling the eye.

It slid forward as if propelled by some inner force, glistening and glinting in the early-morning air like an apparition. It was Ra's golden boat, come straight from the Underworld.

Then I heard the beat of oars. Against the sunlight I saw the outline of oarsmen and saw the sprays of water beads flung like jewels from their paddles.

It was a *real* boat with at least twenty on board and a huge dark red sail embellished with the Double Crown of Egypt. As it came closer, I saw the Eye of

Horus decorating its bow and its name written in hieratic script beneath.

Dazzling Aten.

"Queen Tiy's barge," someone whispered.

I held my breath, expecting to catch sight of her on the golden throne under the red canopy with the wings of her gold vulture crown sweeping the air. Why was she out on the river so early?

But as the barge came closer, I saw it was a man who sat there. By his elaborate dress and spangled leopard skin, I knew he was the highest of high priests, Wosret—the Most Powerful One.

The barge came straight toward the temple jetty. Village boys were shoving and pushing and squabbling to reach out and catch the ropes. The captain stood bare-chested in the prow, wearing a short linen wrap. A gingery beard jutted from his face like a tangled bush and met with the nest of hair on his chest. He wore no wig, and his equally matted red hair fell to his shoulders like a wild cloak and was tied at his forehead with a white band.

All were wearing the same headbands. The white headbands of mourning.

The women began whispering.

"Someone has died."

"But who? And why has *he* come?"

"Yes. Why *him*?"

"What can be so important?"

"Must've been someone really important; otherwise the highest of high priests wouldn't have come here."

I whispered a quick prayer to Hathor—not only goddess of the moon, but also the goddess who carries the souls of the dead to the West.

Servants stepped off the boat and beat cymbals to ward off evil spirits as the highest of high priests was carried ashore in a golden sedan chair encrusted with lapis lazuli and turquoise and jewels of rainbow hue. The sand in his pathway was swept with a date-palm leaf and sprinkled with precious oils as he was set down.

The women fell to their knees.

My father came rushing down the path, already dressed in his temple clothes, a broad gold band around his neck and the gold crocodile bracelets clasping his upper arms. I was pleased I had pleated the linen of his tunic properly and left it under a heavy stone to flatten overnight.

He bowed. "My Lord, Wosret. Most Powerful One!"

The highest of high priests held up his hand and the crowd fell silent. His high cheekbones and strong nose with flaring nostrils gave his face the appearance of carved wood rather than flesh. And his eyes under dark-lined eyebrows looked as if they had been replaced with glass. Jet-black obsidian set in a statue's face. Lifeless as a lizard's eyes.

"Henuka, as her majesty Queen Tiy's trusted priest and embalmer at the Temple of Sobek, I've come to fetch you for a special embalming."

My father bowed. "It must be someone of great importance for you to have come personally, my Lord."

Wosret's eyes gave nothing away. "This I cannot yet announce."

"My daughter is my helper. If the embalming is of great importance, I'll need her assistance."

Wosret's eyes flicked coldly in my direction but moved quickly away again. Despite the sun on my back, I felt a small shiver run through me.

"Then let her hurry. The weather is warm. We mustn't delay. The bodies will not last." He snapped his fingers at his servants and they stooped to lift his chair onto their shoulders once again.

Bodies? I wanted to ask, but my father's look silenced me.

"Never address the high priests personally unless spoken to," he hissed. "Now, be quick. Collect my instruments and resins of myrrh, hekenu, and nesmen and the bark of cinnamon, cloves, and oils. Bring the *Book of Temple Inscriptions*, too. Tie and seal the chest with clay so no one will meddle with it. And pack the ceremonial wig box and my pleated linen garments. Be ready to leave immediately."

I squinted back at him. "What about the crocodiles? The First Moon appeared this morning before sunrise. It's the day of Ritual and offering to Sobek."

Wosret turned in his chair as he was being carried and called out over his shoulder, "Do not delay, Henuka."

My father bowed and smiled, then spoke under his breath. "The Ritual must wait. The demands of the highest of high priests come first. We must attend the embalming and ensure whoever has died has a safe passage to the Underworld."

"Can it be Queen Tiy?"

"Shh, Kara! Hold your tongue!"

I slid a quick look at the barge with its gleaming embellishments. "But that's *her* boat."

"What of it?"

"Why's *he* using her boat?"

"Shh, now! You ask too many questions. Fetch my things. Change into a clean tunic and wash the mud from your feet. Hurry!"

I tossed my head. "I can't help the mud! I've been doing my work."

"I wish your mother were here. Collect my implements and remember—only speak when you're spoken to. Be quiet otherwise. Stand up straight. Keep your head bowed. Don't shrug your shoulders or toss your head if you don't agree with what's said. The highest of high priests, Wosret, is truly the Most Powerful One. Don't be impulsive and say the first thing that comes into your head. Bite back your tongue. Be warned, Kara!"

These words still draw a bitter sigh from me now as I write them. If only I had listened.

3

ANUBIS, JACKAL OF THE UNDERWORLD

The smell in the small antechamber next to the embalming chamber was vile—sickly sweet with undertones of rotting. Even the juniper oil burning in a chafing dish and the cones of perfumed wax could not mask it.

It was a smell I knew well. A stench of rotting entrails, gut, and stomach gases.

The room was small and hot. There was no opening for air save a slot no wider than a hand, quite high up and recessed deep into the thick stone. I felt my stomach heave. I fought the urge to vomit by tying the mask of linen tighter over my nose and mouth and leaned over the chafing dish to inhale the tang of the juniper smoke.

Next to me, the slimy lumps of bloodied organs lay in bowls ready to be washed with palm oil and immersed in special herb solutions. Next to them, the canopic jars were waiting. In the dimness of the antechamber, eyes glowed like hungry creatures waiting to be fed—the four sons of Horus: Hapi, the baboon with yellow amber eyes, waiting for the lungs; Duamutef, the jackal with red carnelian eyes, waiting for the stomach; Qebehsenuef, the falcon with green verdite eyes, waiting for the intestines; and Imsety, the man with blue lapis lazuli eyes, waiting for the liver.

All the organs lay there in the bowls, except for the heart. The heart, being the seat of wisdom, was left in the body. I knew the powerful spells that would be read to implore the heart not to be separated from the body in the afterlife.

My father's instruments lay on the stone ledge still bloody from their work—the hook he'd inserted through the nose to dislodge the brain tissue, the flint knife he'd used to slice open the abdomen, the wooden adze he had used to scrape out the lungs, stomach, intestines, and liver. He would have cleansed the cavity with palm wine and stuffed it with bruised myrrh, cassia, pounded cloves, and salt to dry the body out.

I pressed my cheek against the cold stone wall and waited. Unexpectedly, I noticed a small gap between the stones. By its worn edges I knew someone had peered through this spy hole before. I could see right into the sacred *wabet* chamber, where the embalming was in process. I pressed my eye closer.

The body of a woman lay on a stone slab, surrounded by shaved-headed priests in linen tunics. My father wasn't among them.

The slab was carved in the shape of a lion and sloped in such a way that the woman's feet were higher than the rest of her body. She lay with her long neck hanging over the edge, completely naked, her limbs long and graceful even without fine linen and jewels. She seemed more like a sleeping princess who might wake and bid her guardians out of her way. Yet the bloody cut glowing like a red garnet necklace across her lower stomach showed she was truly dead.

My mouth went dry. This was no ordinary person. Not with that red flaming hair. It hung in a cascade of brilliant auburn that almost swept the floor. Thick and wavy and textured, as if it had seen hours and hours of brushing with oils.

Beneath the woman's tilted head was a stone basin. I knew the last liquid of her brain would slowly be dripping into it from a hole made at the base of her skull.

I could see her earlobes had two holes each. The double piercing of royalty. And there was a ridge on her forehead as if something heavy had rested there.

There was no mistaking that profile and that hair. It was Queen Tiy! The most beautiful queen ever to rule Egypt. She wore the royal vulture crown with its golden discs of the sun god Amun. The most exalted woman in Egypt now lay dead before my eyes.

I'd seen her float past on her barge, wearing robes as translucent as a dragonfly's wings, thinner than gossamer, embellished with dazzling gold sequins, her narrow waist accentuated with broad beaded belts, her long neck hung with necklaces of multiple rows of shimmering beads and gold amulets, sunlight catching stones of every hue on bracelets, armbands, and rings, two tall white ostrich plumes set with gold sun disks on her head making her taller than anyone around her, with the wings of the vulture goddess sweeping back from her face.

Now I was standing closer to her than I'd ever dreamed.

The priests were walking around her body, making incantations and sprinkling it with white powder. The body would rot quickly in the heat. The salt was to prevent this. I knew the body would lie in salt for forty days until all moisture was drawn from it. Afterward it would be anointed with resin and juniper oil and beeswax. Then it would be wrapped in linen with the heart amulet and other precious amulets between the bindings.

Finally, before being laid in her sarcophagus, there'd be the Opening of the Mouth ceremony. Queen Tiy's mouth and eyes would be touched with an adze. Her spirit would then be able to reenter her body and breathe life back into it for her journey into the afterlife.

The entire ritual took seventy days. The same length of time that Sophet, the Dog Star, the brightest of all stars, vanished from the sky. After seventy nights, when Sophet crept back, the Great River would begin to flood and bring down its life-giving black earth. The same time was needed for Queen Tiy to be reborn. After seventy days she'd make her journey into the Underworld.

But now in the gloom of the chamber, my eye picked up a group of figures standing as a pack of jackals on upright legs. They wore terra-cotta masks with pointed ears, fierce-painted eyes, and the sharp snouts of Anubis. They stood nodding their sinister heads and bowing awkwardly as they tried to see out of tiny holes cut into the terra-cotta.

They stood around a second body on another slab. I pressed my eye closer to the gap.

It was a boy. A leopard-skin cloak covered one shoulder and a jeweled broad collar rested across his chest. In the strange greenish light his face seemed bruised but handsome. There was no bowl beneath his head and no slash across his stomach, so I knew the embalming process hadn't begun yet.

An Anubis-headed priest bent over and put an ear to the boy's chest. As he glanced up, the painted eyes seemed to stare directly at me. I jumped back and held my breath. I couldn't risk his catching the glint of my eye at the peephole. I pressed my ear against it instead.

A muffled voice reached me. "His heartbeat is weak. But he still lives."

It was my father's voice. I couldn't stop myself from peeping. Yes, I could tell by the gold crocodile bracelets on his upper arms—it was him.

Another jackal-headed priest nodded slowly. By the leopard cloak he wore, I knew he was the highest of the high priests—Wosret, who had fetched us in the royal barge. "The poison wasn't strong enough!" His voice rasped with annoyance.

Poison? I listened hard.

"You'll have to help him to the Underworld with a small puncture directly into the heart. Nothing more than the thinnest of needles."

"I can't do that!" My father sounded agitated.

"Why not?"

"I'll be judged when I enter the Hall of Truths. When Anubis holds the scales, my heart will measure heavily against the ostrich feather of Maat. My soul will be cursed forever. Puncturing someone's heart is an act of murder."

Murder? My father, a murderer? I swallowed hard and pressed my eye to the spy hole again.

My father was looking down at the boy on the slab. "I can't allow his heart to be punctured."

The Anubis figures—all except my father—clustered together. The masks made their heads look clumsy. Every movement they made was slower than normal. They were whispering and nodding to one another.

The highest of high priests turned from them. He held his head up so that he could look directly at my father through the tiny peepholes below the snout of his mask. "It's been decided. You won't be judged for doing something that is right for Egypt. We can't allow him to live. He's weak. Egypt has no place for a weak king. His brother, Amenhotep the Younger, *must* be king. We can't allow rivalry between the brothers. Now that Queen Tiy is dead, this is the moment for Prince Tuthmosis to die as well."

What? Tuthmosis! My hands flew to my throat. The boy was the royal crown prince! I held my breath and felt my heart pounding. What would my father answer?

"Tuthmosis is *not* weak. He walks with a limp,

through no fault of his own. It was an accident. You know that!"

Wosret stood with his jackal head thrown back. He appeared to be looking down his snout at my father. "No country wants a disfigured pharaoh. His death is right for Egypt. We do this for the love of his brother, Amenhotep, the boy king."

My father shook his head slowly and deliberately. "Amenhotep is as young as the moon. He's *not* the king. He *can't* be king. On this slab is the rightful king. The *real* king."

Wosret flourished his hand. I half expected to see leopard claws showing in place of fingers. "Amenhotep was named after his father. He was the favorite son before his father died. He's young, but it's not Amenhotep who will rule . . . it's *us!* After her husband died, Queen Tiy meddled too often in the affairs of the Temple of Karnak. We can't have that. Amenhotep, the new king, will rule under our guidance."

The group of jackals standing behind Wosret nodded their agreement.

"Thebes is a viper's nest. It's time for change," Wosret snapped when my father didn't respond.

"But not by killing." Now my father sounded impatient.

Wosret shook his head like a dog trying to get rid of a pesky fly. "I am the highest of high priests. I won't take interference with my plans."

There was an intense silence. Despite the heat I felt shivery.

"Surely . . ."

Wosret lowered his head. It seemed as if an animal growl might come from his throat. "Henuka, we can't have dissension. My way is the *only* way!"

"What do you imply?" My father's words were sharp.

"If you disagree with Tuthmosis's death, you'll have to drink the Cup."

"The Cup!" I heard my father's startled intake of breath.

I was too scared even to blink now as I waited for Wosret's answer. He looked directly at my father and nodded, his jackal ears tipping up and down. "It's your duty for the love of Egypt to drink the Cup. Your soul will travel through the Underworld in peace then." He spoke in a deep, flat voice, with a dismissive wave of his hand as if this were a small procedure to be quickly done with.

The Underworld? Suddenly I understood. My father was going to be forced to drink *poison!* They were going to *kill* him. All because he was protecting Tuthmosis. My mouth went dry. My knees turned as wobbly as the time I'd climbed too high in the mimosa tree. My head felt light and strange as I clutched the stone shelf against the wall.

Wosret spoke firmly, as if explaining something to an unruly jackal pup. "Your soul will travel through the Underworld at peace. Anubis will weigh your heart against Maat's ostrich feather and find your heart light with your good deed. Thoth, the scribe of truth and wisdom, will record you as a man of honor. A man to be trusted. A man who has died for his country."

I stuffed my fist into my mouth to prevent myself from crying out. *No! He's not to die! He's truthful and honest. My father needs no judging.*

In the light of the oil lamp I could see sweat gleaming on my father's bare shoulders. He bowed his jackal head so that his snout almost reached his chest. "I have no wish to die."

"Ah, yes . . ." Wosret spoke appreciatively, as if he were about to sip the finest Syrah wine and was holding the glass thoughtfully up to the light before making a judgment. "But I'm the highest of the high priests. Let me be the judge of when you should die. You've done your work well as administrator of Sobek's temple. We'll be sorry to lose you."

Lose him? You're not losing him. You're killing him! I wanted to shout.

"Then why?" My father's voice cut abruptly through the silence.

Wosret shrugged. "It's quite simple. You're not in agreement with us. This is an opportunity to die an honorable death. Kill Tuthmosis and then drink the Cup."

The silence was broken only by the steady drip of liquid falling from the back of the queen's skull into the bowl below.

"Come on, Henuka! Be reasonable! Your journey will be pleasant. You'll accompany the great Queen Tiy, as well as her son Tuthmosis. I can arrange for your burial chamber to be near theirs, right next to King Amenhotep's chamber. It's an *honor* to be chosen. Don't make me use force. Remember, I am the Most Powerful One!"

My father bowed again. "That fact does not escape me! But as a priest so long in service of the dead king, and now his wife, Queen Tiy, it would be more of an honor to be able to continue with the embalming of Queen Tiy. Afterward, if it's your wish, I'll offer myself to the divine crocodile, Sobek, at the temple where I've served her."

I shuddered. What? Was I, as keeper of the sacred crocodiles, going to have to lead my father into the crocodile pit and watch them devour him? Impossible! I was numb with fright.

Wosret answered smoothly. "To die for Sobek won't suit. It'll take too long."

My father glanced at him. "In my experience, death by a crocodile is quick and fatal. It's *never* long!"

"It is not the method I object to, but the *time* it'll take to arrange for your return to the Temple of Sobek. Don't you see? The less that is known of your dissension, the more honorable your death will appear. We'll announce that you were so overcome by the death of both Queen Tiy and her son that you took your own life."

The thought made me light-headed. I was definitely going to faint.

"Grant me one favor."

Wosret sighed. "We're wasting precious time discussing this, when we should be getting on with it. Well . . . what is it?"

"Allow me to complete the embalming of Queen Tiy. It should not be entrusted to a lesser embalmer."

For a moment Wosret seemed to hesitate. He made a delicate vault of his hands, each fingertip touching the opposite one, in a mock gesture of thoughtfulness. The garnet in the massive ring on his right hand was a bubble of blood in the lamplight. His silence held complete power in the chamber. But he knew my father was right. He bowed his head and sighed as if with great generosity.

"Very well. The favor is granted. But you're not to leave the embalming complex for the entire seventy days. The other high priests will fetch the necessary liquids and ointments and oils from the temple. And when the ritual is complete . . ."

My father knelt and touched his jackal head three times to the floor so that I heard the hollow sound of the terra-cotta ears knocking against the stone. "So be it."

What? So be it! Why didn't he fight for his life? I

pulled away from the spy hole and threw myself back against the wall. A bowl of entrails tipped from the shelf. The terra-cotta shattered. Queen Tiy's intestines lay at my feet on the floor among the shards.

There was a moment of complete silence. I held my breath. Then a voice hissed, "What was that?"

Suddenly the door from the wabet chamber was flung open. Two priests rushed in, grabbed me by the shoulders, and pushed me forward into the presence of Wosret. "She's been spying. And the queen's entrails have been defiled."

I couldn't see my father's eyes through the peepholes in his mask. I spun around to face the highest of high priests. "I heard everything. I know your plot. You're asking my father to be a *murderer*. And because he won't agree, you want to kill him as well."

"Isikara . . . keep silent! I beg you."

Wosret turned to my father. "A feisty girl, this daughter of yours."

He walked slowly around me, looking me up and down with his dreadful jackal face. I clenched my jaw and stood up straighter with my arms at my sides, defying him to attempt to scare me with his yellow jackal eyes and sharp jackal grin. I wouldn't flinch.

"Yes . . . a fine girl. It seems a waste to make her drink the poison cup as well." He nodded his head toward my father. "Not so, Henuka?"

My father kept silent. I could feel him willing me to be silent as well.

"You do not scare me, sir!" I spit the words at him.

"Ah, polite, too!" Wosret bowed his jackal head at me. "Yes. It'd be a waste for someone so polite and pretty to die so young."

My father made no reply.

"But there are other options." The highest of high priests grabbed my arms and pulled them behind me while his dark obsidian lizard eyes flicked over me.

I tried to twist free. I wanted to bite his hands but could not reach them. Instead I spit. The glob lay glistening at his feet.

He pulled me around to face him. "What? You've already defiled Queen Tiy's entrails and now you defile the floor of the wabet chamber. Holy ground, already ritually washed. Ground that we brush our footsteps from when we leave. Defiled by a slip of a girl!"

"She's young and thoughtless." I could hear the note of begging in my father's voice.

Wosret stared at me from beneath his jackal snout. "The poison cup is too kind. Perhaps she's better suited to being a slave. Slavery will soon pacify her reckless spirit. Slavery will teach her how to behave. It will soon *whip* her into shape."

The way he said the word "whip" sent a shiver down my back. And already he spoke of me in the third person—as if I were an object and not a person.

I narrowed my eyes. There was no stopping me. "I'll be no one's slave. Least of all *yours!* I would rather kill myself first."

"*That* you may have to do," his voice rasped back at me.

4

THE OPENING OF
THE MOUTH

The sound of footsteps echoed down the stone passageway as the priests left the wabet chamber. Then a clang of metal shuddered through the walls as the door that led to the temple was bolted shut.

I spun around to face my father. "You knew, didn't you? You *knew* about the poison."

My father thrust off his terra-cotta mask. In the gloom his face was pale. He lifted his finger to his lips, then swung open the door to the antechamber and glanced around quickly to make sure no one had remained hidden.

He turned swiftly. "Kara . . . listen carefully! They've gone back to the temple but only for the ritual of collecting oils. You must do *exactly* what I tell you. There's no time for argument now. You must escape."

"How, if they've bolted the door?"

My father put his hands on my shoulders and gripped me firmly. "I said *listen!* If you don't want to be a slave, listen to me. There's a secret doorway from this wabet chamber into a passage. It'll lead you out of here. It's your only chance. But you must take the boy with you."

"You mean the prince? Tuthmosis?" I glanced at his body.

My father nodded. "He's not truly poisoned. As soon as I suspected the murder plot, I prepared another potion for him to drink—one that merely put him into a deep sleep. I planned to fool the high priests. But I was forced to speak out. I *had* to prevent Wosret from puncturing Tuthmosis's heart. The needle would truly have killed him."

"But—"

"Listen!" he whispered urgently. "Outside in the secret passage is the body of a boy who died last night. I arranged this secretly with the help of a few other priests who discovered Wosret's plot and support my view. The boy's body will replace Tuthmosis. The priests will think it's Tuthmosis lying there. Instead, Tuthmosis will escape with you. Later there'll be a chance for him to challenge Wosret and reclaim the throne. But not now."

"But when the priests return, they'll notice it isn't him."

"Not immediately in this dim light. His eyes will be closed. And he'll be wearing the leopard cloak. But you must be quick. Now that you're involved, the plan is even more urgent."

"I'm sorry. . . ."

My father waved his hand to silence me. "You *must* hurry, Kara! You *must* escape. To be a slave to Wosret doesn't bear thinking about."

The walls of the wabet chamber seemed to be closing in on me. I was dizzy trying to keep up with what he was explaining. "You keep saying *me*. What about *you*? I can't leave without you."

"I'll follow. But first, I must arrange the body on the slab. Everything must seem normal when they return. They'll think we're next door in the antechamber. Having the other body in place will give you more time to get away."

"Let me help you. Then we'll go together!"

"No!" he hissed. "It's too dangerous. I'll follow as quickly as I can. Don't worry about me." He gripped my shoulders and pulled me tight against his chest and then released me just as quickly. "Here . . . take this." He removed something from the girdle bag at his waist. "My Senet gaming board. Be mindful of its messages. Now quick! Help me move Tuthmosis. I need his leopard cloak and his broad collar as well."

I wanted to hold on to my father, but he pushed me away and began pulling Tuthmosis upright. "Quickly! Get hold of him now." He ripped the cloak from the prince's shoulders and unclipped the broad collar with its filigree of jewels and gold. "Put your arm about his waist. Get your shoulder beneath his armpit."

The weight made me stagger. I leaned up against the wall to steady myself. There was no time to give my father another glance. He went ahead of me and slid away a stone, opening up a shadowy space lit by a small terra-cotta lamp.

I saw a dark shape lying at the bottom of some stairs. I turned my eyes away so as not to see the face of the peasant boy and concentrated on dragging Tuthmosis down the steps. By the time I steadied him against a wall at the bottom, my father had already scooped up the other boy. He couldn't bid me a proper farewell. Nor could I reach out to him. We were both weighed down by our burdens.

He nodded into the distance. "At the fork, don't take the passage to the right. It leads to the workers' village. Go left. Take the lamp with you. Hurry! Your life depends on it!"

What about a lamp for you? I wanted to ask. But he was gone. I heard the grate of stone on stone as the secret door closed firmly behind him. The sound echoed through the dark space ahead and shuddered through the stone floor beneath me.

Except for the dead weight of Tuthmosis, I was alone.

The air was hot and heavy with a strange putrid smell. There was a sound of scratching noises. Dark shapes scampered into the murky distance. Eyes caught and reflected in the flickering lamplight like red rubies.

They were rats! The whole passage was full of them.

I kicked at a dark shape that scurried by my sandal. Suddenly something flew up at me from out of the darkness. I ducked as it brushed my cheek and skimmed over my head with a high-pitched squeak. A bat!

I grasped the lamp and held it high with my free hand. Clusters of them hung upside down from the ceiling vault like empty girdle pouches. Too many to count. I was grateful I wasn't wearing a wig, that my head had been freshly shaved for the embalming ritual. The thought of hooks from their wings snaring me made me shudder.

"Tuthmosis . . . ?" I bit my lip. Should I be calling him by his name or by his royal title?

"*Tuthmosis*, I can't do this alone. *Wake up!*" My voice sounded hollow as it echoed into the space. I shook him urgently. But he rested like a stone against my shoulder.

I began half dragging, half pushing him. His legs buckled and splayed in all directions. He started to shuffle along like a sleepwalker. The ground was mushy and slippery under foot, slick with droppings. Hardly daring to breathe, I dragged him beneath the silent black pouches and prayed he wouldn't suddenly shout out and disturb them.

Rats scampered ahead of me, the skittering sound of their nails scraping stone. Their menacing shadows with long tails danced around the walls of the narrow passage in the lamplight.

I could hardly breathe. The space seemed to be getting smaller and smaller. The walls and ceiling were closing in on me. Pressing the air out of my lungs. Pressing in from all sides. Suffocating me.

I stumbled down some stone stairs and propped Tuthmosis against a wall so I could catch my breath and listen for the sound of my father's footsteps. But the silence was broken only by the squeak of rats.

What if he didn't follow? What if I could never find my way out?

Tuthmosis began murmuring.

"Are you awake?" His head lolled against my shoulder as I pushed him upright. "I can't carry you any longer. Do you hear me? Wake up!" I shook him urgently and then, without thinking, I slapped him. A sharp slap on both cheeks.

What? Had I lost my senses? He was the crown prince—son of King Amenhotep and Queen Tiy of Egypt. I should've been bowing to him. Yet here I was, slapping him. I could be put to death for much less than this!

I held the lamp up to his face to see if I'd left a mark. Both cheeks were red. His eyelids were fluttering. What if *he* knew?

For a brief moment he opened his eyes and then closed them again.

"No! I beg you! Please, *please*, wake up!"

He finally looked back at me. I held the lamp closer. Beneath the dark lashes and the rims of black kohl, his eyes were a strange shade of . . . blue? "Tuthmosis, can you see anything? Have you been blinded? Your eyes are odd. They're blue!"

He nodded with his lids half-closed. "I know."

"Impossible! Egyptians don't have blue eyes."

He rested his head against the wall and sighed. His breathing became deep and even.

I shook him firmly. "Don't you dare go back to sleep again. We *have* to find a way out of here."

He shivered and started to grumble about something, then demanded, "Are you one of the palace slaves? It's cold here. Fetch my cloak. Where have you put it?"

"I'm not a slave! Listen! Wosret tried to poison you."

He shook his head like a dog trying to shake off water and then turned and looked at me as if he were emerging from a thick mist.

"Do you hear me? Wosret tried to poison you."

"Wosret?" His eyes opened wide. "Don't be ridiculous! Wosret is the highest of high priests. He's my royal mentor."

"Don't you remember anything?"

Tuthmosis frowned. "A ritual. It had to do with my mother's death. Yes. Now I remember. I was attending her embalming. Wosret offered me a chalice to drink for comfort."

"Comfort? He wanted you to drink *poison.* Listen . . ." I told him quickly about my father's replacing the poison with another potion and replacing him with the dead boy's body.

He shook his head. "Impossible! You've made it up. Where are my servants? Who are you? Why should I believe you?"

"Because I'm trying to help you. If it wasn't for my father, I wouldn't be bothered with you!"

The prince lifted his head sharply and glared back at me. "I could have you put to death for treason."

"*Treason?*" I hissed back at him. "I'm trying to *help*! You don't seem to understand the danger. Look around at where you are. Why do you think you're here? Wosret wants you dead. But stay here, then, if you don't believe me. I can't waste any more time. I'll find my own way out."

He gave me an icy look. I bowed my head and went on hurriedly. "I implore you. They'll be coming after us soon. And my father ordered me to do this."

"How do I know you speak the truth?"

"By the white feather of Maat, every word is true. You *must* believe me." I glanced back quickly at the dark passageway. "My father is supposed to follow. But he hasn't. We have to escape before the high priests come after us. Our lives depend on it. But I can't see an exit."

As I swung the lamp higher, my heart jumped. Wosret suddenly lurched up through the flickering shadows in front of me in his sneering jackal mask. Then I laughed as I realized I was staring into the eyes of a painted Anubis on the wall.

We were in a small vault.

"This *must* lead to a burial chamber," I muttered.

"How do you know?"

I pointed at the ceiling. "There's a painting of Nut, goddess of the sky, lighting the darkness. And here on the wall is Anubis touching the mouth of a mummy with an adze. This is the antechamber before a burial chamber . . . before the final journey to Ra. There *has* to be a hidden door. A mouth to the afterlife."

Tuthmosis seemed distracted. He pointed at the floor. "Those turquoise tiles . . . look at the way they're arranged. Three rows of ten. Like the thirty squares in a game of Senet."

"Senet?" I reached into my girdle pouch and brought out the board my father had given me. "My father said this would help. He said to be mindful of its messages."

The cedar-wood box was long and narrow with a turquoise and ivory inlay. On one side was a drawer. I slid it open. Inside were carved agate pieces. Tuthmosis picked up one and rubbed it between his fingers. Then he started to arrange the pieces across the board.

"We're wasting time . . ."

"No, I'm trying to remember something. Senet

is a game of passage. Your father must've given it to you for a reason." He looked up suddenly. "That's it! A game of passage—a journey! The game follows a journey along the thirty squares. Some squares are more important than others. Look."

I held the lamp above the box. Drawings were incised into the turquoise squares and inlaid with ebony. Each drawing was precise and perfect. In one square was the ibis-headed Thoth, in another a figure of a man in a boat with his head turned backward. A frog. A scarab beetle. A symbol for a maze or labyrinth. A symbol of water. In the last square, an image of Ra.

"It makes no sense. It's just a game. We haven't time—"

"Games have a beginning and an end."

"What's that got to do with the tiles on the floor?"

"The floor is a Senet board. See, there are thirty tiles in three rows of ten. We have to find the end square."

"Why?"

"That's where your pieces leave the board. Where you escape to meet Ra. It's marked with the image of Ra. If we find the end tile, we've found our escape."

I brushed aside the dirt and rat droppings with

my sandal and bent down and peered at the squares. "Nothing. Not even the tiniest mark or pattern. This isn't a Senet board. They're ordinary tiles. And I was wrong. This doesn't lead to a burial chamber. We're in a dead end. We've missed a turn. We need to retrace our steps."

"No! Find the Ra square. There are only two possibilities for it. Facing from either end, it'll be the bottom left square."

I gave him a hard look as I traced my fingers around the edges of the left tile in the bottom row nearest me. He was good at giving orders. "See! Nothing, except rat droppings!"

"Try the other side."

I went to the opposite end and held the lamp high. The turquoise color of the left tile was worn. My eyes flew to the narrow, shadowed gap around the tile's edges. Then I caught Tuthmosis's knowing look and was forced to admit, "You're right. This *has* to be it!"

5

THE COBRA
GODDESS

The tile was heavy. Eventually I managed to loosen it and ease it aside. Below was a gap. I held up the lamp and followed rough steps that led into a dark, narrow space. They sloped downward and ended against a stone wall.

"What's there?" Tuthmosis groped his way down the steps toward me. I could see by the way his foot turned in that the bone had set badly.

"Another dead end. The passage is sealed with a stone wall."

He traced his fingertips across the stones and stopped on one particular rock. "There's a pattern here. Lines crosshatched. Like a web. It's a symbol for a labyrinth. It could be a sign. What did he mean?"

I frowned at him.

"Your father. When he gave you the Senet board, he said to be mindful of its messages."

"Oh, that!" I shrugged. "Maybe this is the entrance to a labyrinth." I began to claw at the edges of the stone that was marked, searching for a place to loosen it. "It's useless. My fingertips are bleeding."

"We need something sharp. What do you have?"

My hand felt for my girdle pouch. There was my throw-stick that Katep had carved, but I didn't want it damaged, and my mother's bronze mirror. I'd snatched it up before leaving the Temple of Sobek. The reflecting disk was a large moon held up by Hathor, so that when I looked into it, Hathor's face showed directly below my own. She gave me courage.

"There's this." I drew it out from my pouch.

"You took a *mirror* to my mother's embalming?"

"I meant no disrespect."

He laughed. "My mother would've been delighted. She spent hours in front of her mirror every day while her attendants arranged her face and finery. Now, hurry. Dig!"

I gave him a look. He spoke like someone used to giving orders and having them obeyed. *I'm not your servant* is what I wanted to snap in reply. Instead, I jabbed Hathor's feet at the stone's edge and sent her a silent prayer to ask for help in holding my tongue.

My hands were raw and scraped by the time the stone eventually loosened. I wiped them against my tunic and rubbed the mirror clean.

He shrugged as he saw me do it. "Not quite as perfect as before, but the face that looks into it will still be perfect."

I bit my tongue. He'd given no thought to asking my name but felt free to give me orders and pass comments about my face.

He put his shoulder to the stone and shoved. Then he edged his body halfway through the opening.

I held up the lamp. "What do you see?"

He was silent.

"Tuthmosis . . . ?"

"My father's tomb."

"It can't be."

He turned toward me. "It is! I played here while it was being built. I came when he inspected it with his chief vizier. I watched the vaults being carved into the mountain, the walls being smoothed, the sculptors at work, the artists as they painted, and the scribes writing holy spells on the walls. It took more than ten years. It's *his* tomb!"

I squinted through the lamplight at him. "How can you be so sure? It could be any king's tomb. They all look the same."

He gave me a look. "Do you think I don't know the exact details of my own father's tomb? His sarcophagus is carved of red granite."

I shook my head. "A sarcophagus is *always* carved from graphite."

"His wasn't!"

"Let me see." I pushed him aside and began squeezing through the narrow opening.

He grabbed hold of my tunic. "Stop! Don't dare enter."

"Why not?"

"You'll destroy the tomb's sanctity. My father won't reach the afterlife."

I turned fiercely. "It's our only escape. From the tomb there'll be a passageway back to Thebes, surely. We *have* to enter."

Tuthmosis stared back. In the lamplight his blue eyes reflected like cold moonstones. For a moment I hesitated. Then I tossed my head. "You have to trust me," I said, and as an afterthought I added, "And you might ask my name."

He shrugged his shoulders impatiently. "What is it?"

"Isikara. And you should know—just because you're the son of a king doesn't make me your slave."

Our eyes stayed locked. Then he said my name slowly. "Isikara . . . we both have to learn to trust each other." He turned and went ahead.

I followed him through the opening, edging my way into the darkness, keeping one hand on the wall, feeling the sharp stone under my fingertips.

There in the lamplight stood the silent sarcophagus. My breath caught. The prince had been right. It was red. Red as oxblood.

I shuddered, thinking of what lay inside. The

golden mummy case, and within it another golden case, and another and another until in the final one, the mummy of King Amenhotep, wrapped in the finest of linens, decked with jewels, his arms across his chest holding the golden pharaoh's crook, his face covered with a golden mask, on his forehead the cobra ready to strike.

We were standing in the very heart of the burial vaults of Thebes. Beyond our tiny pool of light, the darkness stretched upward to a ceiling painted deep blue and scattered with stars. Around us, other vast, empty spaces disappeared into thick blackness.

Tuthmosis turned abruptly. His footsteps echoed against some stone steps that led between two huge square pillars into an area with more pillars. I jumped back as King Amenhotep loomed in front of us, staring straight into my eyes. He wore a magnificent girdle belt set with real lapis lazuli and turquoise. A shining gold and obsidian pectoral plate hung against his chest. On his brow was the striking cobra. Written above were these words:

Beware the cobra goddess who guards the royal king
and his treasures. The cobra goddess anoints his head

with her flames. Through her, the terror that he inspires
is made more. Such is her power!

She sat on the pharaoh's brow with her hood flaring, ready to spit poison at all his enemies. Ready to burn them with her fiery glare. But she was a fickle goddess. Not just the defender of the pharaoh. She could be *against* him as well. Her bite could cause the pharaoh's death.

As I stood there, I felt I was calling up her anger. I clasped my arms quickly across my chest and held my hands to my throat for protection against her deadly bite.

"Hurry, Isikara!"

On another wall Hathor was drawing Amenhotep along, wearing an exquisite dress of turquoise beads clinging in a cloudlike net to the curves of her body, carrying the moon on her head, a turquoise broad collar around her neck, flaring cobras with burning carnelian eyes dangling dangerously from her ears. I begged her for protection as I passed.

Beyond her, my eye caught a glimmer and sparkle of things in great heaps in some side chambers.

Tuthmosis saw my glance. "It's my father's treasure. His gold chariot for his ride across the heavens. His gold bark to carry him along the river of the Underworld. His throne embellished with ivory, bloodstones, and lapis lazuli. His gilded cheetah bed. His servants are all there, too, sculpted in terra-cotta, and his gold hunting bow, along with a gold statue of his favorite hunting dog embedded with emerald eyes."

"So much?" My whisper echoed into the dark spaces.

"Even more. Rolls of fine linen, leopard-skin cloaks, gold-bladed jewel-encrusted daggers, headrests made of glass, chests filled with golden goblets, scarabs, amulets, necklaces, bracelets, breastplates, rings set with stones of every shade of the rainbow, alabaster jars filled with the best wine and olive oil and caskets of ox and goose meat. Not just his favorite chariot. More than six chariots. All has been catered for." Tuthmosis nodded toward some paintings of men bearing gifts. "The princes of Syria, Palestine, Babylon, and Nubia lavished him with turquoise, amethysts, perfumed oils, gold, ivory, and skins. And here it all is!" He swept his arm around the darkness.

We entered into a passageway and were prevented from going farther by a well shaft carved into a sharp right turn. The shaft was flush with the walls and wide enough to prevent anyone from jumping across it. Its sides fell straight down into the heart of the mountain. Deep below, I caught an oily black reflection of water. There were no footholds to give access to the opposite side.

"How'll we cross?"

"Stone slabs originally bridged the gap. They've been removed to prevent anyone from reaching my father's treasure. But there's another secret way out. My father sculpted a series of vaults, with sliding doors and secret passageways meant only for his trusted vizier so he could enter and inspect the well and ensure it collected and prevented water from running down the passages into the burial chamber."

"It can't be so secret if workmen knew of it."

"Each team of builders worked on only a section of the secret labyrinth. No one but my father's vizier knew the final plan."

"No one but the vizier and *you!*"

Tuthmosis ducked behind a small pillar. A statue of Anubis glared at us from a niche. A metal collar around Anubis's neck was linked by a heavy chain to a metal ring in the stone floor. The prince pushed against the niche and it swung open.

"A secret door?"

He nodded. "It swings back to rest in place again." He was about to allow it to shut behind us.

"Wait! What about my father? How'll he know it's a secret door?"

Tuthmosis pulled off one of his sandals and wedged it in place so that a small gap showed.

I'd lost track of time. It was hard to tell how long we'd been in the passageways. Perhaps more than a day, even. "My father should've caught up with us by now."

But Tuthmosis was already hurrying ahead. We were in a cavern of chambers with crypts and niches and winding passages leading into darkness in every direction. Our lamp had no way of casting light in such a vast space. Vaults and stairs and images of gods and statues receded into the gloom. Nothing moved. Just deathly silence.

I knew about labyrinths. They were complicated spaces planned to protect burial chambers. Passageways wound backward and forward in bewildering patterns meant to confuse. Doorways showed the way ahead and at the same time tricked a thief to go back along the same passage. Once, Katep and I had secretly entered one but hadn't dared to go beyond the first chamber.

"Which way?" I whispered.

"Here." Tuthmosis guided my hand across a stone wall. I felt three indentations on the corner of the wall.

"I carved these at every point where a decision has to be made. The passageway goes all the way to the Great River so my father's *ka* can escape into the afterlife."

Tuthmosis edged forward and I followed close behind him, my heart thumping in my ears. It wasn't as easy as he made out. I had a moment of doubt each time he felt for the three marks. This wasn't the game he'd played as a child, where he could call out and his father's vizier would come. In the twists and turns of the labyrinth, we could be lost forever.

As we came through a doorway there was a terrifying rumble—as if the entire labyrinth was collapsing. It echoed through the passageways. I clutched Tuthmosis's arm. "What's that? Are we trapped?"

He shook his head and held up the lamp to show me some ropes. "It's a trick to scare thieves. I'd forgotten about it. The sound is made by rocks rolling in a stone jar that falls from a pulley. We triggered the pulley as we passed through the doorway."

As we groped our way along, the air in the passageway suddenly seemed fresher. I knew we were near the end when a scent of papyrus mixed with the smell of sun-baked earth suddenly came wafting toward me. A glimmer of light ahead drew me on. I stumbled ahead of Tuthmosis and began running toward the brightness. It had to be our escape. We were free at last.

I stopped short. There was the opening that would lead us out of the labyrinth, but a metal grid barred the way. I rushed forward and gripped the shiny rods and shook as hard as I could. It felt as if someone were throttling me.

"It's useless!" I shouted over my shoulder. *Useless . . . useless . . .* I heard my voice echo back into the darkness. I sank to the ground. "We're locked in . . . *locked in!* We're here forever . . . *forever!*"

✦ ✕ ✦ ✕ ✦ ✕ ✦ ✕ ✦

6

THE FESTIVAL
OF SOPHET

Tuthmosis came up behind me.

"Shh!" he hissed. "Are you trying to get us caught? Someone will hear you!" He felt along a hidden ledge and brought out a key in the shape of an ankh. "Only my father's vizier and I know about this."

I spun around to face him. "But you couldn't have been *sure* it was there, could you? You took a risk! A curse of locusts on you, Tuthmosis! Why didn't you warn me?" My voice was coming out in gasps. I wanted to shake him.

"I said we had to trust each other." He fitted the key into a lock and turned. The grid swung open. "Now listen! This leads into the grounds of the palace near my father's mortuary temple. We can't stay in Thebes. If what you say about Wosret is true, it's too dangerous. We need a boat to travel upstream toward Nubia, beyond the borders of Egypt."

I shot a look at him. "Nubia? That far?" Suddenly I was fearful. The passageway had been a link to my father. I'd listened for his footsteps, but I hadn't given a thought to what we would do afterward when we escaped. I glanced back into the darkness behind us. I was truly leaving him behind. He'd never find me in Nubia. "Do we have to go *that* far?"

Tuthmosis nodded. "It's the only way to escape Wosret."

I looked him over. "You'll be easily recognized. You'll have to disguise yourself as a girl."

"A girl? Never!"

"A boy with a limp and blue eyes is a giveaway. They'll know it's you. You'll need a girl's tunic and a wig as well as a boat. Can you get that?"

"I know someone who'll help. She's not Egyptian. She came from Mitanni in an entourage of Tadukhepa, the daughter of the prince of Naharin Satirna, who was sent to be my father's wife. We're friends. I trust her. Stay hidden here while I find her."

I shook my head. "I'm coming with you."

"It'll be quicker if I go alone. There are guards and guard dogs."

"I'm not afraid."

After the darkness of the labyrinth, it was like stepping into a strange dream. The sunlight seemed too bright, the air too perfumed with mimosa, and the drone of bees too heavy and loud. In the distance below us was the mortuary temple, its gold walls and silver paving glinting in the sunlight. A phalanx of glistening black granite lionesses led to its silver doors. These were guarded by two colossal stone statues of King Amenhotep. Even from this distance the statues seemed huge.

With a quick sweeping glance, I took in the poppies and cornflowers making splashes of red and blue in the fields, the gardens laid out with date palms, the row upon row of green arbors heavy with grapes, the orchards lush with apricots and pomegranates, the fields of lilies with each bud staked so it wouldn't droop, the roses in every hue from soft cream to flaming orange to a red darker than blood.

Suddenly I realized what I was searching for. People. There weren't any. The entire landscape lay silent. There was no one at the mortuary temple, nor any laborers hoeing or leading irrigation water in the orchards and fields.

I glanced toward the Great River and saw the reason. Even from this distance I could see it was covered with sails wafting back and forth like hundreds of pale butterflies. On the opposite bank, a mass of people was moving along the sphinx-lined avenue that led from the river to the Temple of Karnak. On either side of its gateway, huge pennants of the sun god Amun fluttered from the massive cedar flag posts.

A thrum of music and voices came floating up to us on the breeze.

I frowned at Tuthmosis. Then suddenly I remembered. "Sophet! The Dog Star must've risen! It's the Festival of Sophet! Thebes is celebrating the rising of Sophet and the rising of the floodwaters. Amun has to be thanked for saving the country from famine."

"Even better! Let's hurry! The palace will be empty. Everyone will have joined the procession."

Along the river I saw the red sails of the royal barge. I curled my fingers to my eyes to cut the glare and focused on the figures on deck, scanning them for any sign of my father.

"Do you think he's there?"

"Who?"

"My father."

Tuthmosis shielded his eyes as well. I saw him stiffen. "My brother's on that boat! Curse him! He's already wearing *my* crown—the royal ceremonial Atef crown of ostrich feathers topped by gold Atum disks. Kept only for special ceremonies. All you said is true. Wosret has lost no time!"

The swish of sistrums came to us like reeds brushing in the breeze. But above their music, I heard another sound that sent a shiver through me—an eerie wail of wind as it whistled among the stone cracks of the two statues of Amenhotep. The plaintive sound added its voice to the celebration. Even after death, Tuthmosis's father could still be heard!

We ran between tall papyrus reeds and ducked into the shadows along the walls of the garden. For the first time I saw how scarred Tuthmosis's left leg was, but the rest of his body was well muscled and his limp didn't slow him down.

There was nobody about. Not even guard dogs. I caught glimpses of a menagerie—wild antelope and strange, tall giraffe creatures and lions with huge dark manes in separate enclosures. But there was no time to stop as Tuthmosis hurried me through an elaborate maze of cages. Around us the air rustled and rang with curious animal sounds and eccentric squawks. Brilliant-feathered birds flashed against foliage and monkeys jumped from branch to branch in shafts of sunlight.

Tuthmosis gave a sharp whistle. The creatures fell silent, and from behind a high stone wall came an answering call.

"Who is it?" I whispered.

"It's her. The girl."

"Why isn't she at the procession?"

But Tuthmosis had already disappeared through a gate. I followed him into a courtyard filled with flowers and trees and paintings on the walls of still more flowers and trees. At my feet, rills of water alive with small fish trickled among paving stones painted with even more fish. The courtyard seemed filled with every kind of tree, flower, and creature. There was no way of knowing what was real and what was truly decoration.

But the girl was real. She was quite the most exotic creature I'd ever laid eyes on.

Her linen robe was woven with dyed red threads and tasseled along the edge, different from anything worn in Thebes. And her sandals, made from plaited papyrus, were drawn up sharply in the front in the shape of a boat's prow. I imagined them plowing through the sands of some faraway desert.

Her lips were touched with red ocher and her dark, mysterious eyes were rimmed with kohl, made darker still by the brilliant color she wore beneath her eyelids. Not the usual green malachite eye paste worn at important rituals to symbolize new life, her eye paint was bright turquoise, as brilliant as the flash of a kingfisher. It made her eyes appear even darker— like deep reflecting pools.

In her hand she held a broken sistrum handle in the image of Hathor. Metal disks from the sistrum lay scattered at her feet.

She turned pale at the sight of us. "Can it be? They said you were *dead!*"

She rushed forward and bowed low over Tuthmosis's feet so that the plaited strands of her wig swept into a rill and dragged wet marks across the paving.

He helped her up.

"It's truly you! I can't believe it. People are wearing white headbands of mourning for both you and Queen Tiy! Wosret has announced your death."

"He lost no time!"

The girl nodded. "So much has happened since the sun rose yesterday. The rooms of the Middle Palace are already prepared for your brother even though he still wears the side lock of youth. He's been given the leopard-skin robe of office and today he wears the royal ceremonial Atef crown. The girl Queen Tiy chose before she died will be given the Scepter of the Lily to carry in her left hand today at the ceremony. They plan a royal wedding."

"You mean Nefertiti? My brother is to marry *Nefertiti*? She was chosen for me."

The girl nodded and went on quickly. "Today your brother will be presented to Amun at Karnak. He will be named King Amenhotep the Younger. Everyone has joined the procession. I was late. My sistrum broke—"

"What?" Tuthmosis interrupted. "The priests are going to the innermost sanctuary of Amun, the Most Secret of Places, with *my brother?*"

I knew how binding this was. His brother would be led away from the eyes of the common people through the dazzling painted halls with mammoth columns reflected in the silvered floors, into the sanctuary of the supreme god Amun. A mysterious secret ritual would confirm his new powers. Afterward the statue of Amun would be carried by the priests to the royal barge and taken upstream to the Temple of Luxor. In the darkest recess of Luxor the new pharaoh would meet his royal ka—the spirit of his inner being that ordinary mortals meet only after death.

But a king is privileged. In this secret place Tuthmosis's brother would meet his ka face-to-face and then emerge a god-king blessed by Amun—the sun god's living image on earth. To be obeyed by everyone.

"You *can't* allow this!" The words slipped out before I had time to think.

I saw the flare of anger in Tuthmosis's eyes. "Do you think I won't fight to win my kingdom back?"

The girl shook her head. "You won't win it back.

The priests will *never* let you return. They've told everyone you're dead. They'll make sure you die so their plan remains in place."

"I'll gather an army against them." His eyes were as cold and flinty as river pebbles as he caught my look.

I shook my head. "An Egyptian army against Wosret? The Most Powerful One? Never. Everyone is terrified of him."

"There are armies beyond Egypt's borders. If I can't get the support of Egypt, I'll get the support of Egypt's enemies." He turned to the girl. "I need your silence and your help *urgently*."

"You have both!" Her eyes darted toward me.

He saw her look. "Isikara is coming with me. I owe her father my life. Are there servants about?"

She shook her head. "None. They're all at the procession. The only guards left have raided the storehouse and are already in sodden stupors from palace beer. They wouldn't know the difference between an ox and their grandfathers right now. Without your mother to keep order, everything is upside down. And with the news of your death as well, everything is in turmoil."

"The dogs?"

"Chained up. The guards wanted to be free of bother."

"Quick, then, Ta-Miu! We'll go to my mother's quarters. We're least likely to be disturbed there. Isikara needs a wig. Nothing fancy. Something for protection against the sun, as well as a disguise. I need one, too. One that makes me look like a peasant girl."

I saw the girl try to hide a smile. Ta-Miu? So that was her name. Ta-Miu was the word for "little cat."

"And we need a boat," Tuthmosis said as he turned abruptly and led the way through a massive doorway.

✦ ✕ ✦ ✕ ✦ ✕ ✦ ✕ ✦ ✕

✦ ✕   ✕ ✦

7

TA-MIU, THE GIRL FROM MITANNI

Each room seemed more vividly painted, more glistening with glazed tiles, and more brilliant with inlays of painted plaster than the last. There was too much to take in with a single hurried glance.

I ran breathlessly through the passages lined with decorated boxes, each with a plate naming the papyrus they contained. Many more than in my father's temple library. My eyes swept over the names as I ran.

The Book of Dreams. The Book of the Black-Maned Lion. The Book of Plagues. They were all there. Too many for one man to have ever read in a lifetime.

At the very heart of the palace was an audience room so vast that I was scared to look up. The entire length of its ceiling was painted with the huge wings of the vulture goddess, Nekhbet, and the vault was supported by mammoth columns adorned with lotus flowers unfurling their great petals against the ceiling. Under our sandaled feet, portraits of Egypt's enemies flashed by—trodden on daily by the pharaoh as he passed through this room to his canopied throne.

Beyond this were the royal bedchambers. The girl disappeared down a passageway. Tuthmosis drew me quickly on.

Queen Tiy's bedroom was painted a brilliant red. As we entered, I was overpowered by the perfume of hundreds of lilies filling urns everywhere. Hovering over us with giant outstretched wings was another painted vulture goddess. And snarling up at me with claws bared and terrifying eyes was a lion. I stood paralyzed until I realized it lay flat on the floor without flesh or muscle.

Queen Tiy's feathered vulture crown was right

there before me on a special stand. My fingers ached to touch it, to lift it up and feel the weight of it on my head, and to sense the sweep of its wings glittering with gold and jewels at either side of my temple.

I glanced at Tuthmosis. How did he feel being so close to his mother's things? But he was expressionless, as if passing through a stranger's chamber, and urged me quickly past.

There were cats curled up everywhere. Lying on the drapes that covered a huge lion-clawed bed and sleeping on cushioned chairs. One rubbed itself against Tuthmosis's legs. I saw a faint smile cross his face. "My mother shaved her eyebrows the day her favorite cat died. She had all her cats embalmed after they died and buried them in sacred receptacles."

We came to an inner sanctum. My breath caught. Everything any woman could desire lay waiting for the hands of the queen—as if she were about to walk into the room at any moment.

Small chests, intricately inlaid with ivory and mother-of-pearl, held cosmetic spoons, kohl tubes, eyebrow tweezers, curling clips, combs, delicate glass phials of perfume, and turquoise-glazed offering bowls. Ostrich fans and an array of amulets, bracelets, rings, and jeweled broad-collar necklaces spilled out onto tables, like multicolored rainbows.

Tuthmosis moved around restlessly, touching and moving things. Plucking here and there. Mindlessly stroking a cat that had followed us. "What's taking that girl so long?"

Without being able to stop myself, I dug my fingers into the jewels and brought out a ring with the largest amethyst I'd ever seen. I picked up an ivory comb expecting to feel the warmth of the queen's hand still on it. A single strand of hennaed hair twirled through its teeth. I traced my fingers over a translucent alabaster cosmetic spoon in the form of a girl carrying a gazelle-shaped container. I lifted the finely carved head that formed the lid. When I held it to my nose, the hollowed belly still smelled of perfumed wax.

Just then the girl returned. She took the jar from my hands and replaced it. She handed me a fresh tunic made of coarse, unbleached linen. She moved with the light, quick hover of an iridescent dragonfly. The plaited side pieces of her wig swung against her cheeks like delicate beaded curtains as she offered me a tray of glazed apricots and some thin slices of smoke-flavored duck.

"There's no time to eat," Tuthmosis snapped. "What about wigs?"

The girl opened the catches on a box. "I'd have brought two of my own wigs but they're too distinctive. These are from the servants' quarters. They've already been powdered with cinnamon against lice and perfumed with rose oil."

"Lice?"

"We need sandals," Tuthmosis interrupted.

"I've brought some." She glanced at me. "Two pairs of mine. Your feet are the same size." The ones she held were normal flat-woven ones, not the upturned kind she was wearing. She held some toward Tuthmosis. "And two pairs of your own."

"What about the boat?" Tuthmosis asked.

"There's a reed boat waiting for you at the causeway closest to the south gate. The causeway will take you directly south to join the Great River farther upstream. With luck you won't come across anyone returning from either Karnak or Luxor. There are throw-sticks and harpoon spears in the boat to catch waterfowl and fish. I've put food in a basket as well, and there are skins to keep you warm." She glanced across at me. "And a small casket of almond and cinnamon oil to protect you from the sun and wind."

She'd thought of everything.

"Would you like kohl to protect your eyes from the glare and some of my Syrian eye paste made from ground turquoise powder mixed with almond oil?"

Tuthmosis clicked his tongue. "There's no time for this! They'll be returning soon."

"Wait!" I touched the girl's arm. "I must ask something. Have you news of my father, the priest at the Temple of Sobek?"

She shook her head. But when I searched her face, her eyes seemed to say something else. She shrugged. "No one is sure of anything. There are rumors. One moment it's said we'll be sent back to Mitanni, the next it's whispered we'll all be made slaves to the new pharaoh."

Tuthmosis tugged at me. "Come now, Isikara! We must hurry!"

Suddenly I felt uneasy. Maybe my father would still come. I eyed the prince. "Can't we wait? Just until tomorrow? The sun's already low. The river might not be safe at night."

He shook his head. "We can't risk it. You heard

Ta-Miu. They've already announced my death. They'll kill us if we're found."

Ta-Miu nodded.

I glanced at her. "And you? They might kill you for helping us."

"I'll have to risk it."

"Come with us!"

"No!" Tuthmosis glanced coldly at me. "It's difficult enough to escape with you. But I'm duty bound because of what your father did for me. Three of us would be impossible."

So I was a burden! For a brief moment we stood eyeing each other.

Ta-Miu broke the tension. She reached up to Tuthmosis and put a small, delicate hand on his arm. "Go carefully!" she whispered. I saw her slip something to him from her girdle bag. I noticed the small tattoo on her left shoulder. It was the outline of a cat.

We went quickly down the pathway to the causeway, our footsteps slapping against the stone and echoing in the stillness as we ran.

A tall figure loomed up out of the shadows. "Oy! Stop!"

It was a guard so drunk, he could hardly stand. He came very close and peered into our faces. I smelled fumes of palm wine on his breath. "Where are you going?"

My heart stood still. Tuthmosis had not yet put on his disguise. He'd be recognized. But before we could say anything, the man's legs gave way beneath him. He fell into a stupor at our feet and we skirted quickly past him.

We found the reed boat as Ta-Miu had said and pushed off silently from the bank. The sun was already dropping behind the Theban mountains. I felt my own heart sinking too. Hidden in the mauve shadows beneath the cliffs were the bodies of Tuthmosis's parents—King Amenhotep lying in his red sarcophagus waiting to journey to the afterlife, and Queen Tiy waiting for the Opening of the Mouth ceremony.

And my own father? Was he there too? In one of the passageways, finding his way toward us? I prayed with all my heart that it was so.

I looked back at Tuthmosis. "How far will we go tonight?" I whispered.

"Beyond the outer city of Thebes. We'll be going

against the current, but the wind blowing upstream will be in our favor."

Beyond the outer city! It was a frightening thought. The farthest I'd ever gone was across the Great River to the western bank. Now I thought of Katep. Like him, I was traveling farther and farther away from everything I'd ever known. It wouldn't do me any good to look back. But how could I look forward? What lay ahead was too unknown. The thought numbed me into silence and made the paddles feel like stones in my hands.

The breeze had died. In the slow silver light, the only sound came from the flap of the sail and the swish of our paddles as we urged the boat forward against the smooth-running current. Now and again, the stillness was broken by the splash of a whiskered catfish as it broke the surface to catch a water fly, or the fluster of wings as a surprised heron flew up from the reeds.

A sudden beat of oars behind us made my heart leap. Not a single oar but many. In the purple dusk, I saw a dark red sail and the huge bulk of *Dazzling Aten*, its sharp prow slicing through the water, bearing down on us.

WOSRET

T hey're after us! They know we've escaped. Ta-Miu must have told them!"

"Impossible! Ta-Miu would *never* reveal our secret."

"Then why are we being followed?"

"Someone must have spotted us."

"Paddle faster!"

"We can't out-row them! They've twenty oarsmen and a captain who knows no mercy."

"Stop rowing, then!"

"One moment you say paddle faster, the next you say stop rowing. Which do you want?"

I grabbed the second wig. I already had mine on. "Put this on! Pull the tunic over your head. Quick! You *have* to be a girl now! It's our only hope. They're looking for a prince and a girl. Not two sisters. Don't speak! Don't let them hear your voice. I'll answer for both of us."

The barge was gaining on us. While Tuthmosis arranged his wig and clothing, I paddled closer to the reeds. If we were lucky, they'd pass without seeing us hidden among the papyrus. I turned to inspect the prince. He made a handsome peasant girl. His eyes challenged me to keep silent.

I bit my lip to stop myself from giggling. "Wrap something around your forehead so your eyes don't show," is all I said.

Now the barge was so close, its sails blocked the last light of the sky. With a shudder I saw Wosret sitting under the canopy. Two slaves held flaming torches on either side of him. It had to be serious for him to travel by night. The captain stood in the prow, holding a torch to light the way so the barge would not run into logs and floating papyrus and debris being swept down the river.

We sat quietly, our paddles clenched, holding our breath. For a moment I thought they might pass, but the captain's hand went up. "Hold your oars!" he shouted back to the men, and pointed. "There's something out there! Among the papyrus alongside the bank."

With a sudden swish, all oars came up. The barge glided silently toward us. The captain leaned forward in the prow. His large chest gleamed in the torchlight, and his fiery red hair teased out and lost its edge as it sprouted and tangled with his beard and made a huge lion's mane around his sweaty face.

"Who are you?" His voice boomed over the silent water like thunder.

"Two peasant girls, sir. Come from the Sophet Festival." I did my best to put on a rough peasant accent and kept my head bowed to appear like a humble farm girl. I prayed Wosret would not come up to the prow as well. We were low in the water. From where he was seated under the canopy, his view of us wasn't good.

The captain waved his torch above us. "What

are you doing out on the river at dusk? Are you not frightened of crocodiles?"

"Crocodiles don't scare us, sir!"

"Well, they should, you foolish girl! Why are you returning so late?"

"We've come from the Sophet Festival, sir."

"Yes," he answered testily. "You've said that!"

"Our dog has died. She was trampled underfoot in the crush at the festival. We're here to offer her as a sacrifice to the great god Sobek. As you know, sir, it is said that whoever is devoured by the crocodile god, Sobek, is possessed forever by divinity!"

There was a snigger from one of the oarsmen. "A divine dog!"

"Well spoken of the great god Sobek! How is it that you know so much of him?" The torchlight flickered across his coarse features and wild mane as he waited for my reply.

I bit my lip. I was always saying too much. Speaking too freely. Why couldn't I hold my tongue?

"Captain!" Wosret called out impatiently from beneath the canopy. "Enough of this time wasting! Hurry with your questioning. Make sure they are who they say they are. Then let's be on our way."

"Yes, sir." The captain nodded as he peered across the water. "So where's your dog?"

I hesitated. Tuthmosis crouched forward and whispered under his breath. "Tell him we've already thrown it overboard!"

"The dog is here, sir!"

"Idiot! What'll you do now?" Tuthmosis asked.

The captain held the torch high. A path of gold rippled across to us. "What are you whispering about? Where *is* the dog?"

I grabbed a skin Ta-Miu had given us, snapped the cord that bound it, and gathered it up in my arms, holding it as if it had a dog's weight of muscle and bone. "Here, sir!"

"Well, girl—offer it to Sobek, then! Throw it in!"

"Yes, sir! But I don't know the proper incantations."

"Say what you want. Just get on with it!"

"To the great god Sobek. May he not crush two humble peasant girls between his mighty teeth. May he arise from the water and take our offering that we most humbly and earnestly—"

"Enough! Enough! Sobek has heard you! So have we all! Cast your dog before him now, without further preamble or speech making!"

I hurled the skin bundle into the water on the side closest to the reeds and watched the water take it, praying it wouldn't spread out and float toward their boat into the path of the torchlight. For a moment it seemed to catch the current but then was trapped by a clump of reed. Before they could notice anything suspicious, I picked up my paddle and whacked it down hard and then called back to the captain. "It wouldn't do for a dead dog to drift alongside the royal barge, sir!"

Suddenly Wosret appeared in the prow alongside the captain.

"Who is this girl? How does she know this is the royal barge?"

"I can . . ." I bit my lip. I had almost said *read!* But no peasant girl would be able to read. "I can see by the red sail and the handsome decoration, it *has* to be a boat of some importance!"

Wosret leaned over the railings. He stood twisting his ring and staring at us across the water in silence. I held my breath and kept my head bowed. Next to me so did Tuthmosis.

Then Wosret pointed at him. "That one—your sister—she's a silent one."

"She grieves, sir. The dog was her favorite pet."
I was glad the night air had turned my voice husky.
With my servant's wig and deep voice, I prayed
Wosret wouldn't recognize me—or Tuthmosis in his
girl's tunic and wig.

"Where is your father that he allows two girls
alone on the river at night?"

"Celebrating, sir! It's the Sophet Festival."

The captain nodded. "Drunk, probably! Eh?"

"Maybe so. There's a new king to be celebrated,
sir." I kept my eye on Wosret while I spoke.

"That we know, girl!"

I nodded but kept silent.

The captain held the lamp a little higher and then
turned to Wosret. "Should we take them on board?"

Wosret shook his head impatiently. "We're wasting time. Just find out what they know."

The captain nodded and called down. "We're on
the lookout for two traitors. A prince and a young
girl. Have you seen them come this way?"

"If we'd seen a prince, sir, we'd have followed him.
We're poor peasant girls, sir. A prince would have
done us well."

"Well, watch out for one. Be sure to report to an official if you come across a prince who limps."

"A prince with a limp, did you say? It wouldn't be Crown Prince Tuthmosis, sir?"

Behind me, I heard Tuthmosis's sharp gasp.

The captain shook his head. "What foolish girls you are, eh? Tuthmosis is dead! How else would his brother, Amenhotep, be king? It's another prince we search for."

Wosret snapped his fingers at the captain. In the flare of the lamps I saw his garnet ring clinging to his hand like a bubble of blood. "Let's waste no more time! Darkness is descending. Row on! They can't have gotten far!"

We sat in silence after they passed, until their wake stopped washing against us and our boat finally stopped rocking. The night grew dark around us.

Finally Tuthmosis let out a deep sigh as if he had been holding his breath. "That was stupid, Isikara."

I found I was shivering. "I hate him! I *loathe* Wosret!"

"But you didn't have to taunt him."

"I wanted him to feel guilty."

"A man like Wosret never feels guilt."

"I *had* to say something. He's killed my father! He's made him drink the poison cup."

"You don't know that for sure."

"I *do* know! My father would've followed otherwise. Why else hasn't he? And why else would Wosret be out on the river looking for us at night? They've discovered my father replaced you. You heard Wosret! *They can't have gotten far.* . . . He knows! He's after us! And he's killed my father!"

"But you didn't have to pretend to throw the dog into the river! Now we've lost our blanket!"

"What?" I gasped. "You brute! What do blankets matter when I've lost my *father*? There were *two* in the bundle." I hurled another skin into his lap.

We stared at each other unflinchingly. Then he turned abruptly and reached into the woven basket. He plucked out a flask of sweet fig wine, pulled the stopper with a sharp plop, and drank some. He held it out to me. "Have some of this. You're not yourself and neither am I. Remember"—his voice dropped lower—"I've *also* lost a parent."

I eyed him angrily. "It's not the same for you!"

"How do you know?"

"Because you're a prince!"

"Do princes not have feelings?"

I glared straight back at him. How could he of all people know how I truly felt? I wanted to thump my fists against his chest. Instead I snatched the flask from him, took a quick gulp, and almost choked at its strength.

"There's nothing wrong with me! It's *you* who's strange!" I snapped as I wiped my mouth with the back of my hand. "I'm fine!" But suddenly I felt my stomach heave, and before I could help myself, I was spewing over the side of the boat.

"Isikara?" He put a hand on my shoulder.

I shrugged him off. "I'm fine!"

"But . . . ?"

"Leave me alone." I bent over the side of the boat and spewed into the water again. "I'm just . . . just angry and . . ."

"And what?"

"And . . . perhaps scared . . . ?"

He sat back in the boat and began to laugh.

I looked back at him. "What? Curse you, Tuthmosis! At a time like this, you laugh? You really are a brute."

"Sorry. But I never thought I'd hear you admit that."

"What?"

"Being scared."

"And I thought I'd never hear you say sorry!" I snapped back at him.

"We could've been killed by them. No one would've known. Our bodies thrown to the croco-diles in the darkness. We'd have disappeared forever!"

"So?" I eyed him.

He was looking at me strangely. "But it didn't happen, did it?"

I shook my head.

"It didn't—because of *you*. You managed to bluff Wosret! Have you seen the ring he wears? When I was a boy, he used to tell me that with that ring he had power over everything on earth. He could make things happen. *Anything* he wanted. And I believed him. But you outwitted him. We should drink a toast! We've seen the last of him. The last—until I've gathered my army against him."

"We'll *never* see the last of him!" The bile rose up in my throat again.

Tuthmosis reached out and shook my shoulder.

"Don't say that. What lies ahead will be different. But we'll live the days as they come. My father's kingdom stretches as far as the Second Cataract of the Great River. Beyond that, in the land of Nubia, we'll be free of Wosret. I'll gather an army to fight him. To fight for my crown."

I looked back at him and willed myself to believe in what he said.

We pulled the boat up among the papyrus reeds and spread the skin blanket on top of some grass that lay flattened beneath a grove of palm trees. We took out the dates and millet cake and slices of roast fowl Ta-Miu had packed.

A smell of wood smoke and sounds of drums and rowdy voices drifted back to us from Thebes as we ate. I stood and scooped up some smooth flat pebbles, walked to the water's edge, and flicked them angrily one after another across the water. If Wosret had been there, I'd have liked one to have found his heart.

The stones skimmed the surface and jumped along like agitated flying fish. Even Katep would have been impressed with my skill. But if Katep had been here, I might not have been in this mess.

Eventually, even the frogs fell silent and darkness came down like a star-spangled cloak. Tuthmosis pulled the skin over us and soon he was breathing deeply. I lay and felt for the knots on my bracelet, praying to Hathor for protection. Then I asked for forgiveness as well for twice calling Tuthmosis a brute.

I must have fallen asleep, because later something woke me. There was a swish of grass and someone treading softly but firmly. A huge, dark shape appeared in the long grass. Then I heard a snuffle, the sound of grass being pulled and snapped, and a deep rumble of guts. There was a foul smell.

It wasn't a person. It was a hippopotamus! And it was *very* close. I knew these animals came out of the river at night to feed. We were lying right in its path. I could hardly breathe as I nudged Tuthmosis.

"Tuthmosis!" I whispered close to his ear.

"Wh-what?" He turned over grumpily.

"Shh!"

There was silence as the hippopotamus stopped eating. I imagined its ears swiveling and twitching around to catch the sound of us. One snap of those huge jaws, and we'd be done for!

But the sound of grass being pulled and snapped started up again.

"There's a hippopotamus. Next to us."

"Lie still," he whispered back. "They have poor eyesight."

I lay rigid with my arms stiffly at my sides, too terrified even to breathe, and prayed the grass farther down toward the river was sweeter tasting than the grass we were lying on.

"Tuthmosis . . . ?" I whispered later when I sensed the beast had moved farther away. There was no reply, except the sound of even breathing.

All thought of sleep had gone. I lay with my eyes wide open and watched the moon come up—fuller now than the fine thread I'd seen on the morning that was supposed to have marked the ritual of crocodile bathing at the Temple of Sobek. I'd lost track of the days. But one thing I *was* sure of—Tuthmosis was *not* going to be the best of protectors.

I felt for my moonstone amulet and prayed to Hathor again—this time to ward off evils, not just for my sake, but for Tuthmosis's sake as well.

Then I searched the sky to find the stars that outlined Sah, the hunter with his bow and arrow. Katep's constellation. I willed Katep to be searching the stars as well. To be looking up from the desert in Sinai and to be thinking of me. I thought of my father's words: *If you've learned the constellations and the stars, then wherever you are in the world, you'll never be lost.*

I held on to that thought. I would *not* be lost! Not even in spirit. As long as the hunter, Sah, was in the sky, I was safe. This was just as well, because we were to come across the royal barge again sooner than expected.

9

ESCAPE

We journeyed upstream, driven by the steady wind that blew at our back and a fear that never left us. We were constantly alert and watchful. The thought that at any moment we might suddenly come across Wosret and his soldiers in some lonely bend of river kept us vigilant and uneasy.

Our journey took us past clusters of villages hidden among tufts of palm trees. The mud-and-palm-thatched houses were almost invisible in their surroundings with their walls the exact color of the ground on which they stood. In the fields men hoed in preparation for the floods, and along the banks, women washed tunics and spread them over the reeds to dry.

The river was wide. The broad expanse made our boat seem small and gave us the chance to give other boats a wide berth. We sat low in the water and kept close to the reeds. Crocodiles slithered and plunged from the banks with a splash when we came upon them unexpectedly. But for the most part they lay still as stone, their mouths open and their throats exposed to the sun.

Bubbles on the water and a flick of ears gave us warning of hippopotamuses lurking beneath the surface. When they came up with snorting, angry grunts, we gave them space and sailed quickly past.

Occasionally there were men with plaited fishing nets and spears in small reed boats like ours who waved from a distance but paid little attention to us. The larger boats were too intent on carrying their grain and oil and cloth to the temples along the river to take note of us.

Food was no problem. The reeds were teeming

with every type of waterfowl—duck, wild geese, heron, crakes, and waders that had nests hidden among the papyrus stems. Tuthmosis was good with a throw-stick and spear. Here and there we pulled ashore in smaller villages and traded the mullet and catfish we caught for dates and honey and barley bread.

Once, we came to a village of linen dyers where the river ran red with their dye. Sometimes there were markets where linen and wool weavers and craftsmen made cloths, pottery jugs, bowls, leather sandals, and copper pots. Some merchants offered cones of salt, dried fish, sesame oil, ox hides, cosmetics, combs of ivory and tortoiseshell, rolls of papyrus paper, and fly whisks made from giraffe tails.

Sometimes market attendants walked about between stalls with baboons on leashes trained to catch thieves. The baboons barked and bared their teeth and made me uneasy and nervous about being found out.

For the most part we avoided busy places where there was more chance of our identities' being dis covered by Wosret's spies. We stopped in quieter villages to cook fish and share meals of chickpeas and lentils stewed with garlic and onion over a fire while children played late into the night under the stars.

In the boat Tuthmosis wore only his wrap and refused to dress disguised as a girl. But when there were others about, he put on his girl's wig and drew a cloth around his face to keep his eyes in shadow so their color was hidden. We kept to our story—we were sisters sailing south to discover another life. For the most part Tuthmosis remained silent. I spoke for both of us. We drew no attention to ourselves, and in our rough clothes and crudely woven boat, it wasn't difficult to convince people we were peasants.

By carefully listening to gossip we tracked the route of Wosret. He was traveling ahead of us but was no favorite of the people.

"*Dazzling Aten* passed along the river here."

"The highest of high priests came at dusk. His soldiers moved through our village, eating our food, drinking our barley beer, and threatening anyone who opposed them."

"I heard the commotion from the fields. They held my wife and children captive, searching through the rooms of our house, ransacking our belongings."

"What were they searching for?"

"An Egyptian prince, they say. But they wouldn't

name him. Some say it might even be Tuthmosis."

"But he's dead."

"So they say. But so sudden a death seems odd."

"Did they find him?"

"They found nothing!"

"Have they returned this way?"

"Not that I know. But they could've passed at night while we slept and returned to Thebes."

We heard no further stories, nor did we catch sight of the royal barge the farther south we sailed, and so we believed that this is what had happened. Finally we began to feel free of fear.

Tuthmosis eyed me as we sat in our boat among the reeds one day. "You're accurate with your throw-stick. You hunt like a boy!"

I smiled. In the base of the boat lay two waterfowl. Secretly I was pleased with my stealth. I had come upon a pair of shy green herons with the female on her nest and the male fussing next to her. Before they could fly up, I'd aimed the throw-stick and stunned both birds with one throw. Silence and stealth. Days spent on the river with Katep had taught me this.

I shrugged. "It takes a good stick. My brother,

Katep, carved mine from the rib of a hippopotamus. It's easy to handle. Perfectly balanced. Deadly accurate. See—he made carvings on it of a jackal and snake to invoke their power and help me throw accurately."

Tuthmosis laughed as he ran his fingers over the carvings. "It's not the jackal and the snake that are accurate, it's *you!*"

I felt a blush rise to my cheeks and turned my face so he wouldn't see. I fumbled with untying the sail, my hands made clumsy by his compliment.

Tuthmosis was in a playful mood. As soon as he stepped ashore, he began gathering poppies and cornflowers.

"What are you doing?"

"Wait and see." He sat with the flowers in his lap, first cutting a long length of papyrus stem and tying the end pieces together to make a circle. Then, using thin strands of the papyrus head, he tied and wove leaves and flowers onto the ring. His hands worked easily, deftly twisting olive leaves and white willow and the heads of wild celery and sage with blue corn-flowers and red poppies.

"Where does a prince learn to make flower collars?" I teased.

He smiled. "From the palace serving girls. They sat in the gardens weaving collars for one another." He made some final adjustments and carefully placed it over my head and arranged it across my shoulders.

Then he snapped his fingers. "I forgot! There must be perfume as well." He snatched up two blue lotus lilies from the river's edge and stuck them into the collar. "There!" He stood back, smiling. "A temple goddess."

To hide my embarrassment, I pulled a water lily from the necklace and placed it behind his ear. "You must wear one as well!"

Tuthmosis stood there looking more like a prince than ever before—even without a crown and fine robes. He was handsome without seeming to know it. And his eyes were truly blue. As blue as the lotus flowers he'd picked.

He built a small fire with reed and driftwood while I plucked the two waterfowl and split them open. I scraped out the gall and innards, wrapped them in lotus leaves, laid them in the embers. We ate in silence, listening to the frogs and picking the meat off the bones. Then I lay looking up at the stars with the strong perfume of the lilies about my neck wafting over me.

Tuthmosis held his head cupped in his hands and looked up as well. "I slept like this in the desert when I was a child."

I smiled into the darkness. "Princes don't sleep on the ground. They sleep on gold beds in palaces."

"Believe me, I slept on the ground. I went hunting with my father. His days were free of military skirmishes. Syria, Palestine, and Babylon were already his dominions. He had plenty of time for hunting."

"And . . . ?"

"We raced in two-horse chariots over the floodplains, a charioteer at the reins, the wheels of the cart careering across the sand, my father wearing the blue gold-studded Khepresh warrior crown, targeting antelope and ibex. As we gained on them, my father would draw his bow and add to his tally. Fierce lions and leopards, too. He hunted them all."

Tuthmosis seemed to grow fierce with his words. "You saw the skins on the floor of my mother's chamber. In ten years my father felled more than a hundred lions! He wore the skins as cloaks to show his greatness. So all would know his strength and courage!"

I turned on my side and rested my head on my

elbow to look at him. "And you? Were you coura-geous?"

"My father never gave me the chance to test my skills. I stood at his side while he shot the arrows. When we returned and the pace was slow, he allowed the charioteer to hand me the reins. But I never seemed able to prove myself to my father."

"What do you mean?"

"Everything he did, whether it was hunting lions or building monuments, was *always* to demonstrate how powerful he was. The lavish banquets, the gigan-tic statues guarding his mortuary temple, the sprawl-ing palace, the Temple of Luxor inscribed with his name, were all intended to overawe."

Tuthmosis sat up abruptly and raked some life into the fire. Suddenly there was a bitter tone to his voice.

"My brother, sisters, and I grew up not wanting for anything. Our playthings were made of gold inlaid with precious stone. We had giraffe and cheetahs for playmates. Monkeys were trained to fetch fruit for us from the highest branches of our orchards. Slaves stood by to attend to our every need."

He broke a stick with a sharp snap and laid it

across the flames. "My father was generous, but in exchange he wanted absolute power."

I glanced across at him. In the firelight his eyes sparked. But he sat silently as if searching for the right words.

"Yes . . . ?" I urged.

He shrugged. "His power sapped me. Nothing I did, whether it was driving a chariot well or showing I was an expert marksman, ever made him proud of me. In his eyes, I was nothing. Especially after the accident."

I stole another sideways glance. He stared past me into the fire as if he'd forgotten I was there.

"On a hunting expedition, I fell from the chariot when the wheel hit a loose stone. My leg caught in the spokes as it rolled over me. They thought my leg might have to be amputated. The bone was broken. The flesh wouldn't heal. But I eventually recovered. I've walked with a limp since."

He turned and searched my face as if looking for some answer there. Then he shrugged. "My father wanted perfection. He chose my younger brother, his namesake Amenhotep, as his favorite then."

❖ ❖ ❖

The next morning we set out early, hugging the bank of the river. I found myself humming softly as we sailed. There had been days without news of or sight of the *Dazzling Aten*. I felt light and easy. Free of the threat of Wosret. My mind was far away when a sudden glimmer caught my eye.

A mirage rose above the reeds in a bend in the river up ahead. A tall, hazy shape shimmered in the heat, as if overlaid with gold gauze. A shape with a mast and a high golden prow.

It came downstream directly toward us in the glittering morning light with its red sails slack, driven forward by the fast current and the strength of its oarsmen.

I heard Tuthmosis's sharp intake of breath behind me. "It can't be!"

I sat like a snake charmed into stillness by its master. I knew there was something we should do. But the barge had appeared so silently and unexpectedly in such a deserted part of the river that my body was numb.

The hiss of water against the barge's prow and the beat of oars brought me back to my senses. "We can't fool them a second time. There's no protection of darkness now. They'll easily recognize us. We must hide before we're spotted."

"There's nowhere to hide, except under the water."

"That's it! Take a hollow reed to breathe through."

Tuthmosis frowned.

"It'll work. I've done it before. My brother and I used to play this game. We took turns to see how long we could stay under water." I snapped a hollow reed and passed it to Tuthmosis. "Here! Hurry!"

"What about crocodiles?"

I glanced around quickly and shook my head. "None!" I didn't tell him one of us had always kept watch. Then I slipped over the side of the boat, ducked down, and prayed to Sobek to spare us from crocodiles in exchange for all the times Katep and I had fed his sacred beasts.

I thrust the end of my reed upward and sucked hard. No air came. For a moment, my heart raced. The reed was blocked. There was no time to surface and choose another. Panic was setting in. I blew hard and dislodged whatever had been stuck inside it. Under the murky water I saw Tuthmosis holding his reed tightly in his mouth, his eyes wide open and staring back at me like two silvery-blue fish. He gave me the thumbs-up sign.

There was a muffled swish of oars and a surge of water as the barge beat down on us. My heart was drumming in my head. Or was it the noise of the barge? I held my breath. Would they notice our boat lodged among the reeds? Its fibers were water-soaked and had bleached to a dull gray, and the woven strands were beginning to unravel. I prayed they'd mistake it for debris swept down by the floods.

Yet at any moment, I expected to hear the hiss of a flax rope and the splash and thump of a heavy anchor. Expected to see the dark hull at my side and to be yanked up by my arm.

I wasn't getting enough air. My lungs were bursting. I tried to even my breathing. Under the water Tuthmosis held his hand out with the palm toward me as if telling me not to be in too much of a hurry.

We waited for what seemed like forever. I strained my eyes for the shadow of the boat and my ears for the beat of oars. But this time it was truly only my heart I could hear thudding.

We burst through the surface and gasped for full, deep breaths. The barge was nothing more than a golden dragonfly hovering in the heat haze, far, far in the distance—heading in the direction of Thebes at last.

I spit a piece of reed from my mouth and bellowed after it, "Murderer! Vile murderer! You act divine. As untouchable as a god! But you're *not*! You *killed* my father, Wosret!"

Tuthmosis was silent as he held out his hand to help me from the water.

I brushed my cheeks angrily with the back of my hand, hoping the tears would seem like river water, and stood shivering even though the sun was hot against my skin.

The prince picked a single blue lotus lily and pushed it into the collar of flowers that lay in wet, bedraggled strands around my shoulders. He gave a slight bow. His mouth curved up into a broad smile but his eyes were serious. "To Kara—most supreme waterfowl hunter and deviser of untold tricks!"

10

MIRAGES OF THE DESERT

We came eventually to a lonely part of the river with nothing but high desert sand dunes to our western side and dry, barren, stony ground to the east. Both riverbanks were desolate and empty of palm trees, or villages, or children tending goats and playing in the mud. The landscape was harsh, arid, and unwelcoming.

The next morning I woke stiff and chilled next to huge dunes that rose up clear and cold, almost blue in the early light. There was a smell of wood smoke. Tuthmosis was already crouching over some embers, stirring them back to life. I moved closer and spread my hands out to warm them. The dunes began to glow and take on the color of the rising sun. He handed me a gourd of water he'd scooped from the river. Then he fumbled in his girdle bag and held out some dry pieces of millet bread and a few dried olives.

"I saved them from the last village in case you might be hungry."

I couldn't help smiling into the gourd. "You're suited to the life of a nomad."

Suddenly I saw his face freeze. A movement high up along the ridge of the nearest dune caught my eye. I turned sharply.

Five men on camels were outlined in silhouette against the pale sky. For a moment they stood completely still and silent. I twisted my head from side to side to scan the landscape. There was no escape. They had seen us. It was too late for Tuthmosis to slip on his girl's tunic and wig.

"Bind your head at least!" I hissed.

Just as the sun tipped the horizon, the men began

riding slowly down the slope toward us. As the light caught them, they appeared to be dressed in brilliant metallic mesh, woven with gold brocade that shimmered with every slow, tantalizing step.

But as they drew closer, I saw the motley mix of clothes they wore—the layers of bleached and tattered linen with edges unraveling and cloth more patched than whole, the sleeves that hung in tatters around their wrists, and the head cloths that blew and unfurled in the breeze in teased-out strips. The men were bleached, weathered, and worn to nothing but rags, bone, and sinew. Their dark faces were scorched and lined from sun and wind.

Then I noticed something more fearful—the glint and flash of sunlight on metal. An icy coldness swept over me. The girdles around their waists were stuffed with weapons—jeweled daggers and adzes and bronze sickle swords. And, slung across their backs, were enormous bows and dark-hide quivers bulging with arrows.

I'd never seen desert nomads, but instinctively I knew these were the Medjay—expert bowmen who roamed the deserts trading and slitting throats and impaling people for whatever price or prize.

"Stay silent! Let me speak," Tuthmosis hissed as he straightened up to meet them.

Their leader stopped short of us. His face, half shadowed by his head cloth, was harsh and his eyes dark and unfathomable. Up close I saw the strong jawline and high tattoo-marked cheeks. His head cloth was worn to threads, but the boots sticking out from under his wind-torn cloak came as high as his calves and were made of strong leather and stitched in an intricate design.

The other men were silent. Their reins lay loose in their hands, but their eyes watched fiercely.

The leader's dark eyes flicked over us. "What do you want here?"

"We're sailing to beyond the First and Second Cataract."

"The First Cataract is a long way off. The second even farther!"

"We know," Tuthmosis answered, although I wasn't sure he *did* know.

The man stared back. "Where are you from?"

"A village downriver—"

"Tuthmosis is the king's son," I interrupted. If this man was truly a Medjay, for our own protection, it might be well to tell him we were powerful. Then I bit my lip as I caught Tuthmosis's scowl.

The man turned and looked me up and down with the dark eye of someone used to assessing goods to trade. Then he leaned back on his camel and laughed. But it was a laugh without any mirth. "A king's son in peasant dress. And now you'll tell me you're the king's daughter!"

Tuthmosis broke in. "My sister's confused. We've been traveling a long while. The heat of the sun has touched her. We're peasants."

"What are peasants doing so far from their village? Have you broken the law? Are you fleeing?"

"We told you—we're going farther up the river," Tuthmosis answered.

"To what purpose?"

Tuthmosis was silent.

The man narrowed his eyes as he looked at me and then turned to the men. "Perhaps the girl speaks the truth. Perhaps they're *not* peasants." The other men looked on with hard, expressionless faces. "We'll take them. We could sell them. The pharaoh's son would fetch a good price. And the pharaoh's daughter—"

"No . . . no!" I interrupted. "My brother is

right. I'm confused. I'm certainly *not* the pharaoh's daughter."

He turned back to me and spoke slowly as if explaining to a child. "I know that." He held my eyes. "Because a new pharaoh, Amenhotep, has been elected. He's just a boy. He has no daughter!"

"The new pharaoh?" I stared back at the man. How could he know this already? How had he heard the news on the edge of the desert so far from Thebes? What *else* did he know?

He smiled as he saw my surprise. "We have spies. Perhaps there's more money to be made by selling both of you back to the authorities." He looked between us with an eyebrow raised as if he expected an answer. "Perhaps to the high priests of Thebes? I hear they're keen to find a certain boy and girl who've escaped."

Without warning he reached down swiftly and yanked me up onto his camel and swung me across the animal's back in front of him. And even though I squirmed and fought and tried to pull away, he clutched me and held me tightly against his chest to prevent me from slipping free. The camel protested at this extra burden and brayed like a donkey with a broken leg.

This spurred the group into action. One man beat his camel to make it kneel, then reached across and pulled Tuthmosis onto the front; another scooped up our skin blanket with the tip of his sickle sword and flung it across to Tuthmosis. Another reached down and with a few swift scything movements sliced our boat apart so that nothing was left but a heap of debris stranded on the sand.

Amid a hubbub of braying camels, the men dug their heels into their animals and urged them around. Before I could exchange more than a look with Tuthmosis, we were moving in single file up the dune, the leader in front with me held tightly against him and Tuthmosis riding somewhere behind.

As we topped the crest of the dune, I felt the roughness of the Medjay's rags against my arms and his torn head veil whipping against my face in the wind.

Ahead there was nothing but endless desert.

He pulled off a strip of roughly woven wool from his body and handed it to me. "You'll need this for protection against the sun and sandstorms."

The strip felt greasy in my hands and smelled of goat. But I wrapped it around my head and face to protect me from the glare. From a peephole in the swaddle, all I saw were his sinewy arms and his grimy hands with dirt-lined nails as he held the camel reins and at the same time clutched firmly on to me.

The heat drew a suffocating stench of camel, wood smoke, and sweat from his body. But as we rode into the blinding desert, I was conscious not just of the smell of him, but of the sickle sword that kept bumping against my thigh and the bulge of the dagger that pressed hard against the small of my back.

If only I had paid heed to my father's words. If only I had held my tongue, they might've believed we were peasants. Was Tuthmosis silently cursing me? I twisted and turned to try to get a glimpse of him, but the Medjay's arms entrapped me with as much force as the jaws of a crocodile.

We rode in silence, the sun beating down.

I'd never ridden a camel before. Its gait was clumsy. I discovered in time it had three ways of walking— a stumbling short stride like the rolling of a small boat on a choppy river, a longer stride that seemed to dislocate every bone in my body, and a sudden jerky gallop that felt as frightening as instant death.

All of them were terrifying.

There was no way of knowing what distance we were covering. In the middle of the day we rested in a narrow passage of shade cast by a wind-worn outcrop of rock. The water the Medjay offered from leather skins that hung from the camels' necks was warm and tasted of goat. I glanced across at Tuthmosis, trying to read his eyes. We were silenced by the men whenever we tried to speak.

In the middle of the afternoon, a murky cloud like a dark swarm of locusts gathered along the horizon. I peered out from beneath my swaddle. The camels became restless and the men wound their scarves tighter around their faces and turned their backs to the dark horizon.

Then a hush fell. Silent as a dead man's heart.

A huge, solid wall of dust and sand rolled silently toward us. Then the wind began to gust. Harder and harder. As I peered out, the ragged outlines of the men seemed to be unfurling—their clothes, the torn head veils, the edges of their tunics, unraveling— their shapes disappearing in the haze. Bent over their camels in the murky light, they were ghostly apparitions. I lost sight of Tuthmosis.

With a howl like a raging animal, the storm over-took us. The dust wrapped itself around us and the world turned dark. In terror I buried my head into the Medjay's shoulder and heard him laugh deeply against my body.

Sand stung my arms and legs, my throat choked, and my eyes were blinded. Against his chest, I heard the sound of his heart close to my ear. A sound that should have been comforting but instead was terrify-ing. Yet I knew that had he not dug his fingers into my flesh and pinned me against him, I'd have blown away and been lost forever.

11

ANOUKHET

The storm blew itself out sometime in the night while we clung to our camels. In the midst of it I must have dozed. It was the complete silence that startled me from sleep.

The desert stretched endlessly to the horizon, as rippled as the surface of a river and completely unrecognizable. Strange shapes of rock and bone lay exposed and sand dunes stood where none had existed before.

We'd been riding for a long time when I spotted a dark green speck emerge in the middle of the blinding sand ahead. Green? The sun was surely making me delirious. But it grew larger and larger until shapes of palm trees appeared, shimmering and jumping in the haze.

Spurred on by a sense of water, the camels kicked up sand and began to gallop. The leader gripped tightly to his reins to keep his animal under control while I was jostled and juggled about, terrified I would fall under the huge, pounding leathery feet.

As we rode among tall, feathery palm trees heavy with dates and spreading acacias, children and chickens scattered on either side. Dogs barked all around. Low striped tents with sides tied up on stakes exposed shadowy, mysterious interiors.

The camels laid back their ears and brayed and raised frothing lips to show their teeth, snapping in displeasure, as the men struggled to halt them and prod them into kneeling positions.

The Medjay leader called out to some boys to unload the bags and bundles.

I felt the cool shadows wash over me. In the midst of all the noise and movement, I sat senseless, unable to move. The leader reached up and clasped me by the waist and swung me down, past the snarling teeth of his camel. I pulled free of him, brushed the slimy camel spit from my face with the back of my arm, and ripped the ragged goatskin scarf from my head. The leader threw back his head and laughed. Then he turned and walked toward a tent the other men had entered.

I stood there in the shade. The contrast between desert and oasis was beyond belief. We'd moved from a world of blinding, blistering heat into a cool green space, dappled and dancing with sunlight and shadow. It was like being trapped inside a glimmering piece of dark emerald stone.

Alongside some rocks, a spring of water bubbled up from beneath the sand to form a pool where women were collecting water in terra-cotta jars. Peacocks strutted among them, bringing their own glimmer of green to this already shaded space.

Peacocks? How was it possible?

Tuthmosis stood next to me. I caught his eye. We were both too exhausted to speak. People disturbed by the commotion gathered around at a distance and stared. A little boy touched my hand curiously but was scolded by his mother and shooed back to a tent. The women appeared to be discussing us. When one of them came forward with a gourd of water, I pulled it to my lips so eagerly that the water splashed and spilled onto the sand.

In the shadow of a tent, I saw a girl standing with her hand resting up against the tent pole, the other on her hip, staring straight at us. She was tall, loose-limbed, and dark-skinned. She wore a short, boyish tunic and her hair was wild and free in a tousled mass of dark curls that fell around her face, instead of the carefully twisted and plaited wigs worn in Thebes.

A woman clicked her fingers and said something to her. The girl tossed her head, turned, and went inside, then brought out some bowls on a brass tray. She walked toward us with languid indifference as if no one could hurry her, her upright stance and the way she held her body making her seem defiant. Her tunic was rough and her boots were sturdy and made of leather, held in place by straps around her ankles. Masses of silver bracelets shivered and shimmered against one another, and an array of silver rings glinted on her fingers as she held out the tray.

The bowls were piled high with ripe dates, desert

honeycomb, and pomegranate seeds that glowed like garnets. There was a bowl of water for rinsing the hands, with a small piece of linen cloth next to it. Between the bowls lay a tiny spray of yellow mimosa flowers.

I crammed a piece of honeycomb into my mouth so quickly that the honey had no time to drip, and then I scooped up a handful of pomegranate seeds. The girl's dark amber eyes, deeper than the color of the desert honey, seemed to challenge mine. She refused to look away, and it was only when I felt the pomegranate seeds bursting against my tongue that she turned toward Tuthmosis.

I glanced across at him and wondered what he thought of her. She'd brought the tray of food because she'd been commanded. But the tiny sprig of mimosa on the tray—was that her own doing?

Just then the Medjay leader strode out of the tent followed by the other men. A hawk gripped a dusty linen pad strapped to his shoulder. The bird was tied to his wrist by a plait of fiber that connected to a ring on its leg. This was a wild creature with a fierce eye and a screech that set my teeth on edge.

The man pushed the girl aside and shooed the women back. "Enough! They're not guests!" Then he narrowed his eyes at us. "You've seen the desert. You know what a journey across it is like. If you venture beyond this oasis, you'll soon be lost. If you try to escape, you'll never make it out of here alive. It's a brutal and savage death. Be warned!"

I glanced quickly at Tuthmosis. It was true. The Medjay had made a prison for us without stone walls. There was no way of knowing the direction to take back to the river. There were no paths across the shifting sands. The sandstorm had been treacherous. Death by thirst was a horrible way to die! To be exposed to the burning sun, without water and shelter and any hope of finding some, would be terrifying.

Tuthmosis eyed him. "What's your plan?"

The man shrugged. "You'll remain here until we find the right buyer. Someone who makes a good offer. Someone who wishes to return you to Thebes."

"I thought the Medjays were against Thebes!"

"We're against anyone who wants to take away our freedom. But there are times when it's convenient to make friends with Thebes. She's conquered all her enemies right now. There're not many bargains to be made. But the high priests will be interested to know we have captured the king's brother."

"Tuthmosis is the *true* King. Not Amenhotep, his brother!" I blurted out.

The man eyed me, flint-faced and keen-eyed. "At the Festival of Sophet, it was Amenhotep and *not* Tuthmosis who wore the royal Atef crown."

So he knew everything!

"If we're not sold, what then?" Tuthmosis interrupted, without looking in my direction.

The leader appraised him with a sneer. "A lame person is not much use to us. People who are weak or old are left in the desert to die. There's no place for weakness in an oasis in the middle of the desert."

He turned back to me. "At least a girl can cook and fetch water." His eyes were those of a falcon. A falcon watching its prey. I could hardly breathe.

"Tonight we'll celebrate our safe return. The women will prepare a feast. There'll be music." He turned and smiled at the girl. "Anoukhet will dance for us. I command it!"

She lowered her eyelids with a brief look of loathing, then turned her head away with indifference, as if to study a bunch of dates that hung plump and orange between the fronds of a nearby palm. Just then a dog walked by with a monkey sitting on its back.

"Tss tss!" the girl hissed softly through her teeth.

The monkey turned, leaped directly onto her shoulder, and gazed around, as relaxed as if it had jumped onto a palm frond.

The girl glanced across at me. Our eyes held for a short moment before she looked away again.

Anoukhet. So that was her name. But who was she? And where did she come from—this girl who was a dancer and a tamer of monkeys, who was so fiercely indifferent but who was made to dance at the command of the leader?

12

SCORPIONS
OF SEQET

When three bleating goats were brought to be slaughtered for the feast, I thought of Katep and remembered what I'd wished for the day he'd left. I'd wished my life would change! But I hadn't dreamed it would change so much for the worse.

The throats of the three goats were quickly slit and the blood collected in bowls, and then the bodies were skinned, chopped, and added to pots boiling over a crackling fire. Women were chopping onions and garlic, grinding fragrant leaves of rosemary and crushing cumin seeds and cinnamon sticks in a mortar to flavor the stew. Others were straining fermented barley beer into large terra-cotta jars.

I was made to work alongside some girls grinding flour and preparing loaves of bread. Dogs squabbled around our feet for bits of bone and entrails. Children started a game of wrestling and laughing and throwing bits of dough among us. The girls sweat and worked and cast sidelong glances at me. Peacocks, frightened into the trees by the commotion, screeched and added their own cacophony to the day.

There was no sign of Tuthmosis. It was strange to be separated from him. Then Anoukhet appeared at my side and set to silently kneading dough beside me. Her bracelets chased back and forth along her arms as she worked. Her monkey perched in a palm tree nearby.

After a while she whispered, "He knows everything. He knows exactly who you both are—Tuthmosis and Isikara. He'll be ruthless about selling you back to Thebes when the time comes. Your only chance is to escape!"

I stopped and stared at her in confusion while the girls around us giggled and chatted. Flour had settled on her eyelashes and powdered them white. There was a smear of dough across her cheek, but her expression was serious.

"Keep working!" she hissed. "Don't draw attention to what I'm telling you."

"We can never escape. It's too dangerous. How would we go?"

"By camel. It's the only way."

"But we don't know the desert."

"There's an old camel tender here. He knows his time is up. They'll put him out in the desert soon to die. So he has every reason to leave. He'll take us. He knows the way. He's from Nubia."

"Us?"

She nodded. "I'm coming with you."

"Why?"

"This place is a nest of *scorpions.*" She hissed the word.

I gave her a sidelong glance.

"The Medjay are scorpions! Fast, unpredictable, poisonous! And every bit as deadly! They bury themselves in the sand and shelter under rocks, waiting to do evil. They're the most dangerous inhabitants of this earth. Serpents of the underworld." She drew the wedjat Eye of Horus quickly into the flour with her elbow to ward off evil. "Do you know the legend of the scorpion goddess?"

"Yes . . . Seqet. She walks with the scorpion on her head and opens throats to breathe. She allows us to live."

"But also to *die*! She can paralyze throats. She's a dangerous goddess. She protects but also punishes with her scorpion arrows. Her anger causes death. Her scorpions are vicious. The Medjay are just as vicious. Don't be fooled by them. They strike when you least expect it. They're a plague on this earth."

She spit on the ground. "Naqada is the worst scorpion of all!"

"Naqada?"

"The leader. He'd kill you if it paid him more to do so. He's ruthless. He has trained his hawk to peck out people's eyes. If you see someone blind here, it's because of his hawk. Naqada is as evil as Apep!"

My mouth turned dry. That was a name that should *never* be uttered. God of evil and destruction. God of chaos. Every day he tried to swallow the Sun.

I shuddered. "I beg you . . . *don't!* Don't give the Evil One power by saying his name."

"Like must be fought with like."

"How?"

"Every day I make an effigy of a scorpion from beeswax. The sting of a bee against the sting of a scorpion. I leave it out in the sun on the burning sand so it will melt to nothing, in the hope that Naqada's power will also disappear. But it doesn't. With each new dawn, Naqada's power is restored. So I've given up. The only way to overcome Naqada is to escape him! I've been waiting for my chance. With you and Tuthmosis and the old camel tender, we'll manage it."

I shook my head. Her plan seemed unthinkable.

"Naqada captured me as a child and brought me here from Nubia. I'm a slave. We *have* to escape!" she hissed urgently. "And soon. It's the only way. He'll guard you as closely as his hawk guards him. If he can't find a buyer to take you back to Thebes, he'll do a deal with Wosret. Kill you himself—for a price, of course! Whatever happens, *neither* of you will come out of this alive. You know too much. The high priests can't have Tuthmosis claiming his right-ful throne."

Anoukhet was forming the dough with her hands. The charms on her bracelets—frogs, scarabs, dragonflies, scorpions, bees, and turtles—jangled harshly against one another. She slapped the dough into shape as if it were all she cared about. But her breathlessness betrayed her.

Soon the loaves would be lined up and ready for the baking ovens. The opportunity for talking would be over.

"What must we do?"

"We have to act quickly," she whispered. "Escape tonight!"

"Tonight?"

She nodded. "Leave arrangements to me. The camel tender is ready to set off whenever I say. Tonight, while the feasting takes place, be sure to store some food for the journey. Dates, fruit, olives, and nuts. Whatever you can lay your hands on. Steal a saddlebag to carry it in. Bring a cloak or skin to wrap around you at night. And fill any water skins you find. Be sure to warn Tuthmosis that this is our *only* chance. When I give the signal, it'll be time to go."

I nodded and swallowed. Her plan was drastic, her words dire. It was hard to know whether to trust her, but if we didn't, our fate lay with Naqada. To escape and find our way in the desert seemed less dangerous than staying.

13

THE SEVEN
RIBBONS OF
HATHOR

Shadows lengthened. Huge fires were lit and burning braziers placed along the pathways. I wandered among the tents on the outskirts of the oasis searching for Tuthmosis and found my hand suddenly grasped. It was Anoukhet.

She pulled me quickly toward a tent and lowered the flap. It was hung with colored cloth and spread with woven rugs. Her monkey lay curled up on a goatskin in a dark corner. Thick animal skins were strewn everywhere. A carved box inlaid with ivory and mother-of-pearl held glass flasks, terra-cotta bowls, and alabaster jars.

It seemed luxurious for the tent of a slave girl.

"Have you told Tuthmosis?" she whispered in the half darkness.

I shook my head. "I can't find him."

"They're keeping you apart so you can't plot anything. I'll discover where they've sent him and tell him our plan."

"Be careful of how you persuade him."

"Why?"

I shrugged. "Tuthmosis is a king's son. He's not used to taking orders."

Anoukhet laughed as she lit an oil lamp. "I need no protection. I'm not afraid of him." The light caught a sparkle of mischief in her eyes. "We must get ready for the celebration. They'll suspect something if we don't prepare ourselves." She gave me a critical look. "Your clothes are rough and dirty. Those sandals will be useless in the desert. You need leather boots like mine. We need to look like men, if we're come upon. And your wig is awful. . . ." She pulled it from my head and examined the padding underneath. "And full of lice."

"It belonged to a servant. It was a disguise."

"Wigs are useless in the desert. They're too hot to wear. You'd do better to grow your hair long and let it fall naturally."

I felt the short stubble of hair that had begun to grow on the journey. "That's unheard of in Thebes! Normally my hair is shaved to the scalp."

"We're far from Thebes now." She was emptying water into a large terra-cotta basin. She removed a duck-headed stopper from a blue glass vial and tilted it carefully. A few drops of oil fell into the water. A sweet essence of rose petals, jasmine, oranges, and almonds filled the air. She made me sit and rubbed a thick lather of reed sap mixed with moss over my scalp and worked it in around my temples.

"Keep your eyes closed to stop the soapiness getting to them. This will rid you of any lice that may have escaped the wig and nestled in your own hair."

Her bracelets of tiny creatures jingled and sang in my ears.

"Have you a cosmetic box for keeping oils for

the journey? Galena and malachite pastes made with vegetable oils are needed for protection around the eyes."

"I have turquoise paste."

"*Turquoise* paste?" She paused in scrubbing. "It's not a parade of beauty! This isn't Thebes! Have you ever seen an animal that roams the wild with turquoise around its eyes?"

Then she rubbed my head more vigorously as if trying to rid me not only of lice but also of stupidity. "No! A cheetah's eyes are lined with *black*. Gazelles have *dark* eyes. So must yours be! Black kohl, the gray paste of galena, and the dark green of malachite around the eyelids are for *protection* in the desert . . . not just vanity!"

She scooped up water with impatience and let it run over my head and shoulders and then mopped me with a piece of linen. Then she tipped some oil from another vial into the palm of her hand to warm before rubbing it across my back, shoulders, and arms. Her hands worked roughly but expertly, her bracelets making their own music.

She slipped a fresh robe over my head and brought the ends around my waist. It was long and finely pleated and fell from a knot tied on one shoulder. She shrugged as I examined the finely woven cloth. "You can put on a man's tunic later. Tonight you must be dressed properly to fool everyone."

Then she hurriedly washed and oiled herself before slipping into a short tunic woven with bright-colored patterns. She rubbed palm oil into the wild tangles of her dark hair. It gleamed in the lamplight, and her bracelets shirred against one another as she worked. Then she hung large gold hoops from her ears. I watched as she slipped a small jeweled dagger into a sheath strapped to her hips and patted her hand against it.

She shrugged and laughed as she caught my look. "This is my dance outfit. I don't plan to cross the desert like this! And don't look so fearful—I don't plan to stab anyone, either! Now some eye paste. And since the sun has already set, to wear paste now *is* vanity! But why shouldn't we?" She laughed. "In celebration of our escape!"

She dipped into a jar of gray galena paste and rubbed her thumb over my eyelids. I could smell the sweet perfume of almonds and cumin seeds on her breath as she drew around my eyes with a kohl stick.

"There! Just one more thing." She touched the pair of cowries at her neck, then undid the leather cord and removed one shell. She held it up for me to see the underneath. "It's from the sea. A stone of the water's edge. Its power comes from its eye shape. Its magic is as strong as the wedjat Eye of Horus."

She undid my amulet necklace and threaded the single cowry shell alongside the wedjat. "We'll each wear one. We'll be sisters in spirit."

The two amulets lay against my neck as strange companions. One a natural eye shape all the way from the sea, the other the moonstone eye my mother had given me. They were powerful protection.

"We need headbands." She reached into a leather pouch and took out some red strips. "Tie these around your forehead. The seven red ribbons of Hathor. They'll bind her opposite spirit—the lioness, Sekhmet—and protect us tonight! And we'll wear a piece of linen fastened around the throat as well." She laughed as she grabbed a piece of linen and ripped it into two strips. "Let's wear them all. Red ribbons around our foreheads and linen around our necks. Tonight Hathor shields us! We are protected from her lioness spirit! We *ourselves* are lions!"

She flung back her wild hair so that the red ribbons swirled around her shoulders and picked up
a tambourine, shaking it so that the disks ruffled
against one another and joined the tinkling music of
the silver charms on her bracelets. Then she struck
the tight parchment stretched across the hoop sharply
with her fingers three times. "To sisters in spirit! To
adventures ahead!"

"To our escape!" I said quickly before she was
able.

She flashed a smile and threw her arms around me
and we spun around. "To our escape!" she whispered
against my ear while her small monkey scampered
around the goatskins at our feet. "See, even Kyky is
celebrating." She grabbed my hand and romped until
I was giddy and we fell down on the goatskins.

The music and the lamplight and the prospect of
what lay ahead had set her alight. Her mood ignited
my own. For a moment I could forget. I clutched her
hand and strode out of the tent alongside her.

14

NAQADA

"W"here have you been?" Tuthmosis demanded as we emerged from the tent. He was standing on the pathway between the braziers, his tunic filthy and his arms and legs smeared with dried mud and dust.

"Where have *you* been?"

He flicked his hand over his body. "What does it look like? The Medjay have enjoyed watching a king's son work. I've only just escaped. I've been tending the camels. Tethering them and feeding them and watering them." He shot a look at us. "Not dressing up by tying ribbons and scarves around myself."

He looked me up and down. "Your outfit's not suitable."

"Not suitable for what?" I tossed my head. The red ribbons flew about my shoulders.

"Not suitable for anything!"

I felt my jaw stiffen. "Who are you to say what I can and cannot wear?"

Anoukhet glanced between us. "This is no time to fight. We have to have our wits about us. The three of us mustn't be seen like this together. They'll suspect something."

He turned to her. "Suspect what?"

"Shh! Not so loud! Don't attract attention! Tell him, Isikara. I'll look out for you later. I must speak to the camel tender." She waved and disappeared down a path with Kyky scampering along after her.

Tuthmosis gave me a look. "The ribbons are silly."

"It would be sillier not to wear them! They're to tie up the scorpions of Seqet."

He reached out and gripped my arm tightly.

"Be careful, Kara! Don't you see? The girl's wild.

She could mean even worse trouble for us."

"Ha! *Worse* trouble? What could be worse than knowing we're going to be sold back to Thebes? Or killed here in the desert? What's worse than *that*? She can't get us into any more trouble than we are in already. She's trying to help. She plans to help us escape." I pulled my arm free and stood glaring at him.

"Stop being so headstrong, Kara!" he hissed.

"Well then, listen to Anoukhet's plan!" And quickly I told him.

Darkness settled on the camp with a sky so black, it fell like a thick, heavy cloak across my shoulders—a dark coat spangled with more stars than a sky could surely hold.

Beyond the tents in an open space, huge fires with flames plaiting upward sent showers of sparks into the night. Musicians were already plucking at strings of lutes and lyres. An old man sat tapping a tambourine. When I got closer, I saw he was in fact a young man, staring unseeingly down at the ground. His eyelids were scarred and the eyes behind them milky.

Naqada's hawk? I shuddered at the thought.

Girls sat on reed mats in the firelight, dressed in brightly striped wraps with heavy curved collars of beads about their necks. They wore cones of perfumed wax on their heads and their hair was plaited or hung in ringlets, tied with mimosa blossoms and small beads. Some were playing double flutes while their friends clapped and sang. Every now and again a few jumped up and did a lively dance, the huge gold disks hanging from their ears and the bracelets on their arms glinting in the firelight.

Serving girls whisked among the people with huge reed trays resting on their shoulders, heaped with dishes of goat and fowl, steaming bowls of cracked durum wheat flavored with dried apricots and mint, and platters of honey and figs, barley bread and goat cheese.

Music and perfume and flavors filled the night air until my head felt giddy. I kept to myself—as did Tuthmosis and Anoukhet—so we wouldn't be spotted together. I saw no sign of the leader, Naqada.

Much later, when the feasting had come to an end, a group of men burst into the open sandy space with flaming torches. They tossed them high into the air among one another and caught them again with ease. The eyes of the crowd lost their wine-glazed look and flashed with excitement at this new entertainment. One after another the men extinguished the flames in their mouths, then breathed out again so that flags of fire burst from their throats in a sudden whoosh. The crowd roared.

Then Naqada strode forward. His chest and arms were oiled and gleaming, and he was holding a sharp-bladed sickle sword in one hand. He unclasped his hawk's cord and handed the bird to a fellow Medjay.

As the music grew louder and the beat livelier, he began a wild dance, swirling and twisting and brandishing his sword dangerously close to people at the edge of the circle. I felt a swish of air brush my face. It was a test of skill. One small stumble, one slip, would have had someone's cheek sliced off or neck cut through. And one sharp intended thrust could have found the heart of an unsuspecting opponent.

Someone grabbed my arm and pulled me back. It was Tuthmosis. He drew me deeper into the crowd, away from Naqada.

Naqada was joined by a group of fellow Medjay swordsmen. Now the music was even faster as they danced and reeled about. Pomegranates were hurled into the air and swiftly sliced through by the swirling swords. The crowd cheered as red seeds rained down like garnets.

Suddenly, someone threw up a live fowl. It squawked and beat its wings in surprise at being so high up in the air. With the swiftness of lightning finding its mark and just as deadly, a sword swept upward and decapitated the fowl before it could even start its downward plunge. Blood sprayed in an arc against the firelight. The crowd roared again.

Despite the heat of the fires I felt myself shiver and my fingers searched for Tuthmosis's hand. Across the circle I caught Anoukhet's eyes.

Another fowl was thrown up. And another and another—sliced through, decapitated, impaled— until the air vibrated with beating wings. Heads and feathers flew and blood spurted and spattered and sprayed in all directions. The stained sand became a mess of limp, torn bodies.

Suddenly a shrill alarm call silenced the crowd. It was Kyky.

In the center of the arena, one of the Medjay stood holding her by the scruff of her neck. She squealed and shrieked and struggled to free herself.

Anoukhet screamed and rushed forward, but just as quickly her arms were grabbed by two men.

"No! NO!" she shouted as she kicked and thrashed and tried to bite their hands.

Naqada stepped into the center space. His eyes glinted as he glanced at Anoukhet and the crowd began to chant. Then he nodded at the Medjay to throw the monkey up into the air.

I turned my head away and fought the urge to vomit. How evil could Naqada be? How evil were these people that they could urge him on?

I didn't want to watch, but out of the corner of my eye I caught the blur of a small shape somersaulting upward—its body twisting and turning in midair as it shrieked and attempted to right itself. Naqada's sword flashed as it shot up to strike on the downward fall. But at the last moment, he swept his sword arm sideways and caught hold of the monkey with his other hand. He held it tightly against his chest.

His eyes were as cold as an ax head as he turned to Anoukhet. She stood slack. Helpless, with her arms still held by the two men. I couldn't bear to look at her face.

Then, unexpectedly, Naqada spun around and

tossed the monkey toward me. The crowd cheered and clapped. I clutched the small squealing bundle, not sure what to make of the moment. What would Naqada do next? He had known *exactly* where I was standing. A shudder ran through me at the thought of his eyes picking me out of the crowd.

Suddenly I felt weak. He had done this to show I was his target!

Under the silvery fur, the monkey's heart throbbed wildly against my fingers. Then in one violent struggle Kyky pulled free and leaped into the branches of a palm tree. I caught Naqada's horrible smile. I sensed the message in his eyes. I *wouldn't* go free. He clapped and ordered the musicians to play.

"Dance for us now, Anoukhet!" he demanded.

She looked at him with the loathing one might reserve for a writhing snake. Then she shrugged off the hands of her keepers and stood upright and defiant.

"Do you hear me? Dance!" he bellowed again. "Naqada demands it!"

In silence she took one step forward. Someone tapped a tambourine tentatively. It was the blind player. A lyre was twanged and then more lyres and tambourines, flutes and drums, joined in. Slowly at first, then faster and faster, as if beckoning her.

She stood at the edge of the firelight with her hands on her hips, raking her eyes over the faces around her. Then she tossed her head and began her dance—every movement exaggerated, as if she were throwing her anger at the crowd. She spun and whirled and stamped and kicked until her body was a blur. When the music could no longer keep up, she threw herself forward and somersaulted over and over, faster and faster, around the circle of people.

The crowd clapped and shouted, not sensing her display was one of defiance and disdain for them all—but *especially* for Naqada.

Finally she landed in front of him so that the sand flew up in an arc. Her breath came in gasps and sweat glistened on her skin. She stood glaring at him like a wild cat. I bit my lip and prayed to Hathor she wouldn't do anything foolish.

Then she patted her jeweled dagger and spit into the sand at his feet.

For a moment I saw Naqada's hands clench and his eyes glint furiously, but then he threw back his head and laughed. Anoukhet turned away sharply and strode off.

15

THE HEAD SCORPION

We did as Anoukhet told us. We gathered water skins and goatskins and rags of wool and found leather boots as well. After the night of celebration and drinking, the people of the oasis were not too fussed about where they discarded their possessions. It was easy to find a pair of boots that fit and clothes that would keep us protected on the journey. Wherever we could, we stuffed our pockets and girdle bags with dates and nuts and crusts of bread. I found a whole uneaten fowl lying in a dish of spiced sauce and wrapped it in palm leaves and slipped it into a saddlebag.

We were assigned no tents, so Tuthmosis and I found reed mats and pulled them up against a clump of palm trees at the place Anoukhet had suggested. Then we settled down to wait until the camp grew quiet and it was time to leave.

We whispered back and forth but soon Tuthmosis was asleep from exhaustion. I sat awake, hugging my knees to my chest, glad that we would be gone by dawn. Glad that Naqada would soon be out of our lives.

As time wore on, I began to get restless. The fires around us died down but still Anoukhet didn't come. As the shadows closed in, so my own thoughts seemed to close in as well. The smallest rustle above me in the palm leaves, the slightest movement of shadow, set my heart thumping. A feeling of dread came over me.

Where was she? What was taking her so long? Soon the sky would be streaked with light. Then it would be too late.

I leaned across to see if Tuthmosis was still

sleeping, then got up quietly so as not to disturb him and went in search of Anoukhet.

It was hard to recall which tent I'd been in that afternoon. In the moonlight the camp seemed different and the paths confusing. With the flaps down, the tents all looked the same. My footsteps fell silently on the soft sand. Here and there dogs lay growling at one another, gnawing at bones and licking platters. From a tent nearby came heavy sounds of snoring, and somewhere a baby cried but was soon shushed quiet again.

If I could find Kyky, I'd find Anoukhet.

But it was the outline of Naqada's hawk that I spotted first. It sat tied to its perch outside a tent, its feathers silvered by the moonlight. On the other side of the tent fabric came the sound of a muffled struggle. I stole to the side farthest away from the hawk so the bird wouldn't alert anyone and strained my ears. Naqada was in there—I could hear his voice and the sound of his laugh. There was a girl's voice, too, but it was muffled, as if something was being held, or had been tied, over her mouth.

It was Anoukhet. I was sure of it!

I slithered onto my stomach against the sand and

edged a piece of the tent flap slowly aside. I peered into the shadowy space and waited for my eyes to get used to the gloom. Against the tent fabric, I saw the outline of Naqada. He had his back to me and was leaning over someone. By her wild tousled hair and the tinkle of bracelet charms, I knew it was Anoukhet.

He had tied the neck scarf meant to ward off the terrors of Sekhmet so tightly over her mouth, she was barely able to utter a few grunts. Her wrists were bound behind her with the red ribbons.

"So you thought you could mock me in front of everyone? A lesson must be learned. Do you remember Seth, god of the desert? Can you remember what he did?"

Anoukhet shook her head from side to side and kicked her legs.

Naqada laughed. "Yes. I see you do. It was Seth who gouged out the eye of Horus."

A strange sound came from Anoukhet. I felt my own breath pull in sharply.

I saw Naqada grip her more fiercely. "My hawk is waiting outside. All I need do is snap my fingers and she'll do my bidding. You've seen how it's done. You should've known not to make a fool of me. You've been defiant too long. Now you need punishing. After this . . ."

His threat hung in the air. Anoukhet gave another muffled cry.

A blind anger rose inside me. It swirled like a sandstorm in my head until I thought I would choke. My jaw clenched. I slipped under the tent flap.

Over Naqada's shoulder I saw Anoukhet's eyes widen as she saw me. She gave a choked cry and then looked away quickly, to prevent him from following her glance. She made small anguished sounds. Her head strained and jerked in a certain direction. It made him laugh all the more at her helplessness.

I followed the direction in which her head moved. Lying just beyond her reach, on some goatskins, was her jeweled dagger. Its blade was unsheathed. Naqada had clearly wrestled it from her.

I crept toward the dagger with the stealth of a lynx creeping up on its prey. The goatskins softened any sound. I reached and clasped. Then with every muscle tensed I turned and sprang at Naqada's back in a rage. A sound more like that of an animal came from my throat. I gave no thought as to what I was doing. There was no time to think . . . or know what I was planning.

I have no recollection of plunging the blade into his back. I meant to stop him. That's all. To hold it at his throat, perhaps. But in my fury, as the weight of my body fell against him, I brought the dagger down against his back.

The tip punctured his lungs. Found his heart.

He gasped. A low cry came from his mouth. His arms flayed backward, and he slumped down with his cheek against the reed mat. For a moment I thought he was trying to fool us. Then I saw how completely still he lay. I saw his dull eye staring unseeing back at me.

Blood flowed from his mouth, pooling on the reed mat. The silvery light had turned it black, and the black was everywhere. Spattered against the tent fabric. Running down his back. Seeping out from under him. My hands were covered with it.

Suddenly someone was at my side. I spun around, fearing the worst. But it was Tuthmosis. His face was a mask in the strange light. He tried to ease the handle of the dagger from my clenched fingers. I realized I was still clutching it and flung it from my hands. I rubbed them against my tunic as if in the wiping I could wipe away all that had happened.

"I've killed him." I stared first at Tuthmosis and then at Anoukhet. I waited for someone to say something, unable to believe what I'd done. "I've killed him, haven't I?"

Neither spoke. Tuthmosis eased me up. I was drained of all strength. My hands hung limply at my sides. My legs were slack; I could hardly stand. Tuthmosis stooped forward and dragged Naqada aside. He slashed the bindings on Anoukhet's hands with the dagger and cut the gag on her mouth. For a moment his hand rested on her shoulder. "Are you harmed?"

She shook her head and rubbed the marks where the linen had dug into her.

Tuthmosis nodded, turned to me. His eyes were flinty in the moonlight, his jaw hard-set. "He deserved it!" was all he said.

I thought of the heart that had beaten against my ear in the desert storm. I thought of it still and soundless now. I began to shiver. I hugged my arms to my shoulders and shook uncontrollably as I stared from one to the other. The three of us were bound together now. Tuthmosis and Anoukhet had witnessed me murder a man. We were bound as securely to one another as if we'd pricked our fingers and written what we knew of one another in blood and then buried the papyrus.

It was a blood bond as strong as any I'd had with Katep. This was a secret we would have to honor.

Anoukhet stood up abruptly. Shrugged. With that gesture, she seemed to put it all behind her. She gave one last look at Naqada. Kicked at his legs. "Take his sword and his boots, Tuthmosis. They're fine leather and too valuable to waste on him." Then she turned to me and put her hands on my shoulders. "You're not to blame. I would've done it—if he hadn't wrestled the dagger from me. He planned to set his hawk on me."

There was a fearless look in her eyes. But all the same, I knew she thanked me.

We moved quickly then. There was no time for stopping. We gathered our things and found the old camel tender waiting with two camels, as promised. We left the glowing embers, the scavenging dogs, and the upturned pots, passed below the last palm trees, and galloped into the dark night with nothing but the stars reeling out overhead.

There was no longer any moon. What happened to it? Where was Hathor now?

We faced the desert, with Sophet low on the horizon and Sah the hunter and his three belt stars guiding us south toward the river. I prayed that these were enough. I prayed Katep would watch over me. I prayed the discovery of Naqada's body would come long after dawn—long after the Medjay finally roused themselves from their wine-soaked slumbers.

By that time we would be far on our journey.

+ × + × + × + × +

16

INTO THE DESERT

We rode by the stars in silence—each with
our own thoughts.

The old camel tender was up front
with Tuthmosis behind him, followed by Anoukhet
and me in disguise—dressed as men in ragged robes
and long leather boots with woolen scarves about our
faces to keep off the cold desert air, swords hanging
from our waists.

The jeweled dagger I'd not been able to touch

again. But Anoukhet had wiped it clean against her thigh and tucked it back into its sheath at her hip.

The fact that I'd killed a man was trapped in my head like a buzzing fly. I couldn't shake free of it. Was it wrong to kill a man who was truly evil? I was tired, my head dizzy. Every part of me ached. I leaned against Anoukhet's back and allowed the roll of the camel's gait to lull me to sleep.

I woke with a jolt when the movement stopped. We had come to a standstill. The stars had disappeared and the sand was just beginning to gleam and change color in the early light.

The camel tender nodded toward an outcrop of rocky cliffs rising pale and chalky straight out of the desert. "That's what I've been heading toward. The cliffs will provide shade and protection when it's too hot to travel, while we wait for Ra to carry the sun across the sky. I know this place. There are deep crevices where we can hide from the burning sun."

"From the Medjay as well?" Tuthmosis asked.

The camel tender nodded. "That too."

"Scorpions of the earth! We'll fight them if they come after us!" Anoukhet spit into the sand from the height of the camel.

My throat was parched. The sun was just beginning to rise and dust dervishes were already whirling along the horizon. High above us two dark specks floated on the warm air currents. Vultures. Perhaps an omen? I thought of Queen Tiy's vulture crown with its sweeping wings, resting on its stand in Thebes, and whispered a silent prayer to the vulture goddess. "Protect us from the Medjay. Spread your wings over us."

We headed toward the cliffs. They rose in long, fluted columns smoothed and twisted into strange wind-torn shapes with jagged edges and holes worn by scouring sand. Between them, a gap made a natural passageway.

We turned off the passageway and went up a rocky incline that took us into some deeper clefts. The camels planted their feet obstinately and started up a cacophony of moans. Urged on by the old camel tender, they eventually heaved us up with their splayed leathery feet spreading to get a grip, braying and complaining all the way. At the top he tethered them in the shade. They settled on their knees and were silent at last while he began unpacking the saddlebags.

Anoukhet fiddled with something under her cloak and tipped some water from a goatskin into her hand.

A pair of small, troubled eyes peeped out from a fold in the coat.

Tuthmosis gave her a sharp look. "You can't have brought it!" He pulled her cloak aside.

Kyky sat clinging to Anoukhet with a dark, surprised face.

"How can we travel with a monkey? You should've left it behind!"

Anoukhet glared at him. "What? Left her to have her eyes gouged out by Naqada's hawk? Or her body impaled in a frenzy of swordplay? Never!"

"A monkey needs feeding and water!"

"So?"

"Our supplies are limited."

She gave a shrug, as if there was nothing to be done about it. "I'll give up some of my share!" Then she turned and sat, petting and stroking Kyky's head as she stared out across the desert.

Tuthmosis glared at her back, then finally sighed and turned away.

I walked to the edge of the precipice and looked out at the vast sea of sand stretching in all directions.

"Stand back from there, Isikara!" Tuthmosis commanded.

I gave him a look. He was jumpy. We were all jumpy.

We sat in a dark patch of shade where the crevices were so deep that in contrast to the chalky rock, the shadows seemed purple. We took small sips from the goatskin water bag and ate the scraps of chicken I'd brought in silence. From time to time I glanced toward Tuthmosis. But he wouldn't meet my eye. He seemed angry. Restless. What was he thinking? That I was a girl who had killed a man?

I glanced across at Anoukhet. She was silent and seemed oblivious of us. She tore delicately at the chicken bones with sharp white teeth, like a gazelle nibbling the leaves from a bush. When she finished, she held out her fingers for Kyky to lick, then wiped them on her robe.

Suddenly the camel tender lifted his head. He cupped his hands to the side of his face and focused far into the distance. I looked to where he was looking. There was nothing but heat wavering across the sand.

"What? What can you see?"

"They're coming."

"The Medjay?"

He nodded.

Tuthmosis stood up to look. The camel tender pulled him down quickly. "Don't break the silhouette. Keep in the shadow. The Medjay have very good eyesight!"

I made a funnel with my fingers to focus on where he was pointing. All I saw were ribbons of swirling heat vapor, writhing and floating and dissolving far in the distance. I glanced back at him. "Are you sure?"

He pulled his lips into a toothless smile. "I've not survived all these years in the desert for nothing. My eyes see what they see. There are five men. All of them Medjay."

"Five?"

He nodded.

Tuthmosis looked impatient. "How do you know they're Medjay?"

"By the glint of their swords."

"Scorpions!" Anoukhet hissed.

I stared into the distance. I could hardly make out outlines, let alone the glint of swords. They were just shapes swirling and writhing across the horizon like trails of bleached cloth. There was no substance to them. Nothing anchored them to the ground. They simply floated closer and closer, dissolving and reappearing like apparitions in a dream.

A feeling of dread came over me. Even in the bone-dry air I felt sweat begin to prickle and break out on my skin. I dared not close my eyes as I watched the shapes forming and reforming. "What will we do?" I whispered. "Can we outrun them?"

"Ha!" Anoukhet's dark eyes flashed at me from the shadows. "And let them see we're cowards? No! We'll fight them. We have our swords and daggers."

Tuthmosis shook his head. "We can't fight them. They outnumber us. And if we make a dash for it, we'll never outrun them. With one man to a camel, they're lighter and will be much faster."

The camel tender shook his head. "We must do none of those things."

We all turned to look at him. "Then what?" I asked.

There was a canny look to his eyes. "I know the Medjay. I know how their minds work. They'll be in a hurry. In the mood for revenge. For an opportunity to slaughter. We have to outwit them."

Slaughter! A shiver ran through me. Visions of swords slashing, bones crunching, and blood spurting everywhere came to me. I felt the hot stickiness of the word. The butchery of it. The blood seeping from it.

"How'll we outwit them?" Tuthmosis asked.

"By staying exactly where we are—hidden in this crevice high up in the shadow. We have the advantage. They have the sun blazing into their eyes. They won't pick us up in the shade. They'll pass through the passageway looking straight ahead, beating their camels in their hurry to catch up with us. They won't know we've stopped. They think we're on the run. Heading straight toward the river, by the quickest route."

Tuthmosis seemed unsure. "It's quite a chance."

The camel tender nodded. "Our *only* chance!"

Anoukhet shook her head as if we were all mad. "We must face them and fight."

I glanced at her. *She* was brave enough. In her tattered cloak and shredded headband and long leather boots, she seemed as much a warrior as the Medjay themselves. But I knew *I* wasn't brave enough!

I turned to the camel tender. "They'll see our tracks. They'll see we've climbed up here."

"What tracks? Look at the sand below." He pointed to the passageway. "The wind has already smoothed them away and the rocks show nothing of the camels' footprints." He shook his head. "They're not following our tracks. They've come this way because it's the quickest way to the Great River."

He was right. There was no sign of where our camels had walked.

"What if a camel brays just as they're passing? Can we tie up their jaws?"

He laughed and shook his head. "Camels like to chew. If you tie their jaws, they'll bellow more furiously." He drew a leather pouch from the folds of his clothes and reached inside it. "I'll give them dates. They love nothing better than the sweet stickiness to chew on. That'll keep them quiet. Now get ready. Whatever you do, don't stand up. Don't break the silhouette. Stay in the shadow!"

"Ha!" hissed Anoukhet with exasperation. "We're cornered here in this crevice. Let's face them in the open."

She began gathering her things together and wrapped Kyky in a bundle of cloth and handed her to me. I held her, not sure why I was being asked to.

The Medjay were closer now. The camel tender was right. There were five of them racing toward us with their cloaks flying out behind them—all heavily armed. The image of them carved itself into my eye. In the vast, empty space where nothing else was moving, they appeared more menacing.

They were coming after *me*.

I was the one who had killed Naqada!

My heart thumped in my ears, mingled with the drumbeats of the camels. They were so close now, I could see the foamy spittle flying from the camels' mouths and hear the men grunting.

They entered the passageway. There was a movement at my side. I saw Anoukhet crouching like a leopard ready to leap—the dagger in her hand—waiting for the moment they would pass exactly below.

I tugged frantically at her arm. She shook me off. Suddenly, there was a blur of movement. I expected to see her flying through the air. But it was Tuthmosis who had flung himself at her. With a dull thud he wrestled her down to the ground, clamped a hand tightly across her mouth, and pinned her with the weight of his body. Then he tried to wrench the dagger from her. She thrashed and rolled and kicked and struggled beneath him.

They were still in the shadow but dangerously close to the edge. In panic I let go of Kyky and grabbed hold of Anoukhet's boots, clinging to her legs.

Then I glanced down over the edge. The moment had passed. The men were through the passageway and galloping away from us. The noise of their camels had masked the sounds of our struggle. My heart seemed stuck somewhere. I could hardly draw breath.

"Vixen!" Tuthmosis let out a sharp curse as Anoukhet kicked violently and twisted out from under him. There was blood dripping from his hand.

She leaned up against a rock, panting and glaring back at us, her breath coming in gasps, her hair tangled and her eyes glinting dangerously, her teeth and mouth blood-smeared. More wild animal than girl.

"Cowards! All of you! It would've been better to die than to do nothing!" She spit into the sand. "Curse you, Tuthmosis! Why did you stop me? I'd have killed them all. Killed the first one I landed on. Then taken on the other four easily."

"You could never take on four men. . . ." But I was silenced by her withering glance.

"You haven't seen me! I'm deadly accurate with a

throwing dagger. And my sword would have finished off the other three!"

I stared back at her. Yes. With her wild animal face, I could believe she'd have finished them all off!

"I had it planned," she said between her bloodied teeth. "How dare you, Tuthmosis! How dare you stop me! You think because you're the son of a king, you have to be obeyed. I'm *not* one of your slaves. I will *not* obey you! Don't *ever* do that to me again!"

Tuthmosis stood glaring down at her. "Don't ever *bite* me again!" was all he said.

I looked from one to the other as they stared at each other with blazing eyes, waiting to see who would turn away first. When neither did, I stepped between them and took Tuthmosis's hand. "Let me rinse this and bind it for you, before you lose too much blood."

The three of us were tied by bonds, but this was still going to be a difficult journey.

17
ABU ISLAND

When I had finished binding Tuthmosis's hand with strips of torn linen, he nodded toward Anoukhet. "Her hair needs cutting. She has to look like a boy. Yours is short enough. But cut hers."

"Don't you dare!" she growled at me.

I eyed him. "Stop giving orders, Tuthmosis! There's no moss to wet it with and make a lather. It can wait until we reach the river."

"Do it now—without lather. Before we risk meeting anyone else."

I drew my blade reluctantly from my belt.

Anoukhet jumped up. "I'll do it myself!" She snatched up her dagger—the jeweled one that had cut to the heart of Naqada—grabbed a fistful of her hair, and hacked it with one quick movement. She flung the hair down and hacked again and again.

The long black tendrils fell against the sand in shapes as intricate and intertwined as strange hieroglyphs. They seemed to be telling their own secret story—something of who Anoukhet really was.

A new person stood before us, wild-eyed and shorn. I glanced at her face but she wouldn't meet my eye. I gathered up the thick strands and shook them free of sand. How long had they taken to grow to such a length? I laid the strands in a roll of cloth, bound them up, and handed them to her.

She shrugged her shoulders and tossed the bundle into her saddlebag. I saw the glitter in her eyes. I knew they weren't tears of regret, but tears of anger that she'd been forced to obey Tuthmosis. Yes, it would be a difficult journey.

Our camel was a bony and supercilious beast with

bloodshot eyes. We knew the camel hated us from the moment we had first walked around it, wondering where and how to climb up. It had moaned and spit and snarled as we'd approached. The only way to mount the camel without help was to get on while it was kneeling down and then get it to rise.

We heaved ourselves on and sat astride, with Anoukhet up front. She prodded and urged the camel up. In the standing process, we were thrown backward and forward twice—each jolt more violent and unexpected than the one before. Once we were up, if we moved in the saddle, he snarled and tried to snap at us. And when Anoukhet tried to urge him in another direction, he turned to bite our feet.

She seemed not the least bit bothered as she forced it forward down the cliff path.

After a long, silent afternoon of never-ending sand dunes rippling toward the horizon, I sensed the camel's sudden change of pace. Suddenly we came over a rise of amber sand and found ourselves looking down on a landscape of black boulders tumbled and glistening in the sun like polished jet.

The Great River lay before us—but different from

any part of the river I'd seen so far. Instead of smooth-flowing water, the river was choppy and white-curdled as it rushed and tumbled over, around, and between huge, smooth black rocks.

Upstream was an island, so large it seemed almost like the opposite bank. It divided the river in two. The island was rugged and high to the south with stone walls of a temple and a coastline of creeks and small sandy beaches. Groves of palm and mimosa and castor-oil trees came down to the water's edge on the side closest to us. In its heart were tilled patches of cotton plants, lentils, durra, and wildflowers.

The camel tender indicated with his chin. "Abu Island—Elephantine Island—named after the boulders, which look like the backs of elephants wallowing in the water."

After the harshness of the desert, it was like a green jewel set in the river. I let out a sigh. "We're safe at last!"

Tuthmosis shook his head. "Not yet! We aren't beyond the control of Thebes. My father built that temple and a harbor for his army. There'll be Egyptian soldiers here. We must travel farther south."

My heart sank.

Anoukhet shook her head. "We can't move on directly. We need to cross to Syene first." She indicated the opposite bank of the river. There was a sprawl of mud-brick houses with dark-mouthed alleyways between them. "There'll be food and a chance to rest."

"There'll be soldiers as well! It's too dangerous. They'll be on the lookout for us."

Anoukhet laughed as she gave him a swift glance. "Not looking like that! You hardly look like a royal prince! Besides, there's no settlement farther south of these cataracts for a long while. There'll be no market-place or chance of food farther on."

We urged the camels onto a barge that took us to the other side. The bank was crowded with people, bales of goods, heaps of dates spilling out of woven baskets, and donkeys and camels both laden and unladen. Rotting, half-sunk boats lay poking out of the mud, and dried-out hulls lay among the reeds in the afternoon sunshine. The edge of the river itself was covered with boats moored so tightly together that they made a solid raft over which people crossed and recrossed as they loaded and unloaded goods. Men paddled from shore to shore in small reed boats, dragging fishing nets.

The noise of barking dogs, shrill voices, camels snorting and snarling, donkeys braying, dealers shouting, and children squealing and splashing mingled with the hissing and chatter of the cataracts.

Down narrow alleyways people held up goods at arm's length, begging us to stop and look and buy. What was offered was new and strange compared to what I'd seen before. Ostrich eggs, tortoiseshell, porcupine quills, claws and teeth, spears, bows, arrows, ebony clubs, daggers, wrinkled animal skins, whips made of hippopotamus hide, ivory bracelets cut in solid circles from elephant tusks, gold nose rings, leather girdles decorated with bright glass beads and cowrie shells, human skulls—or so they looked—and sloughed snakeskins.

Powerful and exciting aromas rose up from heaps of red, gold, and amber powders, curious-looking roots, shriveled pods, and strange bulbs, and young boys ran alongside us offering handfuls. Anoukhet leaned down from the camel, laughing and arguing, touching and feeling and smelling everything that was thrust toward us. When a boy handed her a flask of castor oil, she pulled out the stopper and began rubbing her arms with it. Then she laughed and handed him a strip of a goat's-wool scarf in exchange.

"Stop that!" Tuthmosis hissed. "You're behaving like a girl!"

She flashed a look at him. "You forget. I *am* a girl! This is my place! I know how to behave here! It's *you* who is the stranger in Syene. You forget I'm Nubian. I'm named after the goddess of Nubia—Anoukhet—goddess of the hunt and goddess of the waters of the Great River! Syene is my home."

"I'll be off, then," the old camel tender announced, looking between the two of them. "You've no more need of me. I brought you safely through the desert; now I must leave you." He nodded toward Anoukhet. "Keep your camel. I'll take this one in payment."

We bade him farewell and Tuthmosis slid down and untied his saddlebag. It seemed to amuse Anoukhet that we rode on the camel while he walked alongside us.

He caught her look. "We'll be selling your camel soon. We need to buy a boat to go farther downstream."

Anoukhet shook her head. "Have you seen the cataracts? Boats aren't used on this part of the river. Camels and donkeys transport everything around the cataracts." She nodded her head toward one of the shadowy, dark alleyways. "There's a place down there to get food and drink."

Tuthmosis shook his head. "It looks rough. There might be soldiers from the garrison."

Anoukhet flashed a look at us and laughed as she made the camel kneel and tied it to a post. "So? We're not girls, remember! I'm thirsty and hungry. Come on," she urged. "Let's not argue about this."

"Aren't you going to search for your family?"

"They're dead, for all I know. They were all taken into slavery. Sold or made to work in the quarries cutting stone for obelisks and statues for the likes of the wealthy pharaohs in Thebes."

She didn't glance at Tuthmosis, but I knew the barb was meant for him. She took Kyky out from under her wrap and placed her on her shoulder.

Tuthmosis glared after her as she marched down the alleyway. "You'll only bring attention to us with that animal."

"There'll be more than monkeys in here to attract attention," she said as she ducked through the doorway.

18

ENCOUNTERS

The rowdiness and noise of the room hit me as we entered. When my eyes got used to the gloom, I saw the area was full of soldiers. They were a rough-looking bunch, disheveled and unshaved. Serving girls moved swiftly among them carrying trays of sweetmeats and palm wine. They were dressed flamboyantly in bright wraps with swathes of beads around their necks and gold trinkets swinging from their ears, laughing and shouting and flirting as they moved about.

Tuthmosis pulled me back. "It's too risky."

Anoukhet laughed. "What? Are you scared?"

"I'm not scared. But the soldiers make it risky," Tuthmosis snapped as he turned to go.

I touched his arm. "We can't split up now. We've traveled so far together. We won't stay long. We'll have something to eat and drink and be off." I glanced at Anoukhet. She was talking to a girl who was stroking the monkey and tickling her neck.

"What's its name?"

"Kyky," Anoukhet replied.

Tuthmosis tugged at my arm. "Come! We're leaving!"

But at that moment two more girls sidled up on either side of us, obviously thinking of the money we might have to spend.

"I'm . . ." I couldn't think what to say. "We're hungry and thirsty! We've ridden through the desert."

"Straight from the desert! But you're *not* Medjay! Not with your foreign accents and fine manners," one of the girls said.

She clicked her fingers at a girl passing by. "Bring

some food and drink for these poor boys before they faint."

I smiled and nodded. The palm wine ran down my throat like fire. I choked and spluttered. "I need water."

"Poor baby! Too young for palm wine." She tousled my head and laughed.

"Leave the boy alone!" Tuthmosis snapped.

She looked at him with flashing eyes. "Don't come in here and order me about."

Tuthmosis pulled her roughly aside. "I said, *leave* him be!"

"What's it to you?" she demanded.

"He's my younger brother!"

"Don't think you can come in here in your smelly, filthy clothes and put on airs and graces far above yourself and then hand out orders as if you're royalty." And with her free arm, she swung back and punched him hard in the stomach. It was so unexpected that Tuthmosis crumpled forward.

A group of soldiers gathered about us— sunburned men with bloodshot eyes. But they were well muscled and despite the rough wraps wore sickle swords in their belts. I could see they were foot soldiers of the Egyptian army. They looked hardy and used to sleeping out in the open on rough terrain. Used to protecting themselves in all situations. Not men to be trifled with.

I shrank back but there was nowhere to go.

They formed a circle and eyed us. The room fell silent.

One, who stood a head taller than Tuthmosis, narrowed his eyes and turned to the serving girl. "Is he giving you trouble, Maya?" And without an answer he took a swipe at Tuthmosis's head with his fist and felled him. There was a bloody gash on the prince's temple, and as Tuthmosis staggered to get up, the soldier swung back his boot and kicked him hard in the stomach.

"Stop!" But before I could do anything, Anoukhet was at my side.

"Let's go!" she hissed.

Between us, we dragged Tuthmosis upright and shouldered him toward the entrance, with Kyky jumping up and down and shrieking and the sneers and curses of the women as well as the soldiers at our backs.

We crept into a secluded side alley next to the

marketplace. I held Tuthmosis's head in my lap while Anoukhet went to fetch water from the river. He lay without moving like when we'd first met in the labyrinth. Except now it was entirely my fault. He'd been protecting me.

Anoukhet returned and wrung out a cloth in the water she'd carried in her goatskin. She laid it across his forehead while I bathed the blood from the wound. "They'll come after us, won't they?"

"I doubt it."

"Why not?"

"I settled it. I gave the girl I was talking to a gift. She'll protect us and see we're not followed. She promised to distract them."

"What did you give?"

"My hair."

I squinted back at her. "Your hair? Why?"

"She'd guessed I was a girl. When I saw there was going to be trouble with the soldiers, I made her promise not to tell we were girls. In exchange I gave her my hair to sell for a wig. They won't come after us."

"She took more than your hair."

"What do you mean?"

"Your silver bracelet with the animal charms is gone."

For a moment Anoukhet looked startled as she glanced down at her empty wrist. Then she shrugged. "No matter! If I'm to be a boy, it's better I don't wear trinkets. But as soon as Tuthmosis recovers, we must move on."

"Do you think his wounds are serious?"

"There's more blood than true damage. The cut's not deep but he'll have a couple black eyes. The soldiers will recognize us."

"It's *all* my fault. He was protecting me."

✦ ✕ ✦ ✕ ✦ ✕ ✦ ✕ ✦ ✕ ✦

19

SERPENT OF THE DESERT

We slept in a doorway that night huddled together among the debris of broken pieces of pottery, mud bricks, and chicken bones. But it was a restless night with soldiers brawling, Tuthmosis groaning, and Kyky screeching every time a dog came sniffling or a rat ran by.

The noise of Syene woke me long before dawn. Tuthmosis stirred and moaned and complained of a terrible headache. I went down to the river to fetch water to bathe his wounds.

The market was already busy even though it was hardly light. Girls still slow with sleep were setting out cucumbers and pomegranates and newly baked cakes on mats on the ground. Between them were jars of goats' milk covered by pieces of goatskin still shaggy with hair. A sleepy-eyed child was sprinkling water to settle the dust.

But it was the presence of the army that caused most of the hubbub. Under awnings strung with lanterns, skin merchants were scraping fresh hides, cutting them, and stretching them over frames to make into shields. Ironmongers, already black and sweaty, were casting molten liquids into molds around their fires. An array of spearheads and arrowheads lay in the sand and the air was filled with the hollow chime of anvils tapping off rough iron edges.

Some soldiers were encamped at the water's edge. In the pearly light, I scrutinized their faces to see if I recognized any of them. It was hard to tell. Going about their ordinary tasks, they seemed different from the brutes of the night before. Some were having their heads shaved. Others were sharpening swords.

The smell of bread baking and the aroma of sizzling meat made me hungry. But I knew it was unsafe to linger, so I pulled my cloak about me, scooped water, and left as soon as I could.

"The camel's gone," Anoukhet announced as soon as I reached the doorway.

"Gone?"

"Stolen. One of us should've stayed awake to keep watch." She took the water skin and began swabbing Tuthmosis's face.

"You hated that miserable camel anyhow!" Tuthmosis squinted up at me through swollen eyes. He attempted to smile but ended up grimacing with pain.

With his hand still bandaged from Anoukhet's bite and his face bruised and battered, he looked quite a sight.

"We'll need donkeys to get beyond the cataracts," Anoukhet said as she dabbed gently at his face. She seemed to be trying to make amends with Tuthmosis. "We can hire ourselves out to load goods that have to be transported upstream. No one will think to look for the prince of Thebes on a donkey!"

A hubbub of shouts coming from the market-place and a fearful drumming of boots against stone at the end of our alleyway silenced us. Each soldier carried a copper-bladed spear and shield. In their belts were axes and swords.

"What's happening?" Anoukhet asked a passerby.

"Some Medjay rode in from the desert last night. They told of three felons who stole two camels and escaped after murdering their leader!" He spit in the sand. "*That's* no loss! But there're whispers that one of the felons is none other than Prince *Tuthmosis,* son of King Amenhotep."

"What?" I couldn't resist. "I thought he'd died and his brother ruled in his place."

The man shook his head. "It's said not. There's a rumor of skulduggery."

"What sort of skulduggery?"

The man drew the wedjat Eye of Horus in the dust and looked over his shoulder. Then he came closer and whispered. "No one knows the truth—Syene being so far from Thebes. The news we get is muddled. But they say there was a plot afoot to have him murdered."

"To have *who* murdered?"

"Prince Tuthmosis. It's said he didn't die of natural causes. It's said the high priests of Thebes were involved in the plot. They preferred the younger brother so they could mold him to their wishes."

Tuthmosis pulled his head scarf lower. "You can't believe rumors." But after the man left us, he scrambled up. "We can't stay a moment longer. We have to move quickly."

Down at the river the donkey men looked askance at us and laughed. "What? The three of *you*? We need strong-muscled men to shift the weight of the loads, not mere *boys!*"

Each one we approached had something disparaging to say, and they laughed directly at Tuthmosis when they saw his face. "Two black eyes! Been in a brawl, have you? We need tough workers here, not boys who are so easily knocked about. And not one with a limp like yours, either!"

I saw Tuthmosis's face drain and saw him clench his fists. I thought he might lash out and urged him on. His misfortune was in truth our good luck, as his two black eyes made him not so recognizable.

Kyky ran ahead, chasing lizards basking on the rocks in the sun and snatching up beetles that scuttled out of plaited mats or sacks being unpacked.

A man loading up his donkeys stopped to laugh at her.

"Have you any work?" Anoukhet asked.

He eyed us. "Come back when you've grown a little."

"I'm strong!" Anoukhet said angrily.

The donkey man shook his head and laughed as he bent down to pick up a huge sack, as if to demonstrate his own strength.

Suddenly Kyky screeched. Anoukhet spun around, clutching her dagger, and threw. My heart stopped at the sound of it flying past my face. I expected the man to fall dead at our feet, the dagger straight through his heart.

But instead he jumped aside. Only then did I see what had happened. Lying right at his feet was a terrible-looking snake—long and scaly, with two horns that stood up behind its vicious eyes. It stared at us through narrow, black, vertical slits, while a thin, dark tongue flicked.

I leaped back as it suddenly flung its coils forward. But the snake was impaled. Anoukhet's dagger had pinned it firmly just below the base of its skull to the hard clay of the riverbank. Its coils twisted and thrashed uselessly.

"A horned viper—one of the most poisonous snakes in Egypt!" The man sounded shocked.

Anoukhet snatched up the dagger from the flesh of the snake and, in one swift stroke, sliced through its neck—so fast that the snake scarcely had time to recoil its body before its head lay separate on the ground, the rest of its coils still writhing.

I gaped at her, then found my voice. "It could have struck you!"

She kicked the head aside and gave me a scornful look. "I'm not frightened of snakes. I took a dare once. I allowed a snake to bite me."

"To bite you? Why on earth?"

"For a bet. I held it for a count. But before the count was finished, it struck."

"Was it poisonous?"

"I didn't know at the time. I watched the poison travel in a red line up my arm."

"And then?"

"I waited to die. But I didn't."

I stared back at her. Was there nothing she wouldn't do?

She shrugged. "It was a dare. I've come across plenty of horned vipers in the desert. They lie in ambush, waiting for their prey under a rock. They sidewind and dig into the sand so only their horns show."

She'd used almost the same words for the Medjay: *They bury themselves in the sand and shelter under rocks, waiting to do evil.* She'd been speaking of Naqada then. The same dagger that killed the snake had killed him. I thought of the rearing cobra dangling dangerously in Tuthmosis's father's tomb. I prayed for Hathor's protection now—Hathor, protector of women, goddess of the moon.

Anoukhet cut a thin, precise line down the belly of the viper and eased the flesh away from the skin with the tip of her forefinger. Her hands worked quickly and accurately.

The man found his voice. "You struck like a bolt of lightning. How did you know the viper was behind me hiding under the rock?"

"Kyky warned me. I heard the scraping sound of its scales before I saw it. A viper rasps them together as it coils back before a strike. You disturbed it when you crouched next to the rock."

"Praise Horus! I'll take you on. We need someone who's fast with a dagger. There are thieves and felons here alongside the cataracts. There's been a murder, they say, and three felons are in Syene, ready to do murder again. Anyone as skilled as you with a dagger will be good to have on the donkey trail."

"Three murderous felons, you say?" She laughed and threw the flesh of the snake to some dogs, who began to scrap over it immediately. She nodded toward us. "What about them? Will you take them on as well?"

The man eyed us and then shrugged. "There'll be no pay except food."

Anoukhet stood up and wiped the blood off her hands. She meticulously rolled the viper skin into a coil and put it into her saddlebag. Then she met his eye with a casual glance, but I saw the curve at the corner of her lips. "That's enough!"

"Well, get to it fast, then, and load the donkeys. We need to leave before the day gets too hot. But first, here—eat some food for strength." He handed us some bread, an urn of buttermilk, and a handful of dates.

The buttermilk slipped down my throat as sweet as honey.

Perhaps it was Hathor who'd sent Anoukhet to us.

The bags of grain were heavier than I imagined and the donkeys we loaded them onto seemed too small for the weight of them. But the boat was eventually unloaded and ready to be hauled empty up the river by the Nubian slaves.

We were already on our donkeys in front of the loads when we were stopped by two soldiers. For a moment as they eyed us, I thought they'd order us down. Tuthmosis had pulled his head scarf around his face. It hid his swollen black eyes. I prayed Anoukhet would be silent.

The donkey owner spoke up. "They're just boys helping me transport this load across the cataracts. I hired them not for their muscle but their cheapness."

The soldiers nodded and passed on to the next group. I caught Tuthmosis's look and smiled back at him.

It was too hot to hurry the donkeys. A dry wind had sprung up and blew the dust around us in eddies. Flies buzzed around our faces, drawn by the sweat of the donkeys. Along the rocky path lay the whitened bones of some poor creature. Perhaps an ailing donkey too tired to take another step?

We went up a rise alongside the river. From here I got my first view of the landscape of Nubia. Under a sky hazy with heat, it had a brassy appearance. In front of us lay a golden yellow plateau of sand. Beyond this were jagged peaks and twisted ravines and a confusion of black rocks and savage-toothed hills that seemed like metal cast and beaten by the sun.

It stretched into the far distance in a purple blur—like a place of utter despair that once I'd entered, I'd never return from.

Eventually we lost sight of the river and came to a hard, flattened landscape where we rested under some scraggy thorn trees. Later the sun dropped away and we happened upon a group of traders whose music and singing drifted to us through the smoky green evening light. Around their fires, groups of men and a few grunting camels, donkeys, and shaggy black goats were sharing whatever meal there was.

We off-loaded our donkeys and sat to one side of their circle.

A man tapped lightly against a hide-covered tambourine that made soft jingling sounds, and he sang in a quiet, plaintive voice. A boy played a reed pipe alongside him. Anoukhet strolled across to them. She sat wordlessly in the sand, picked up the boy's flute, and put it to her lips and began to play.

The thin reed music quavered through the air. And the man's voice rose and fell with sounds that

seemed not to come from his throat, but from somewhere deep inside him, filling the night with unknown
longing.

I looked across at Tuthmosis. Then I reached into
my girdle bag and drew out my father's Senet box.

"Will you teach me the game?"

We laid out the pieces and settled down in sand
that still held the warmth of the sun. We played until
the coals burned down and the night turned grape
blue at our backs.

✦ ✕ ✦ ✕ ✦ ✕ ✦ ✕ ✦

20

THE BELLY OF STONES

We had been traveling with the donkey men for more than a moon along the Great River when we reached the Second Cataract and the forts of Semna and Kumma. The forts of Buhen and Askut had been left far behind. We were beyond the reach of Egypt.

The donkey owner was impressed by our work. To dodge the eye of Egyptian soldiers, we'd volunteered for extra duties that kept us out of sight. The other donkey men thought us too shy to join them when they went off drinking in the markets. But our experience in Syene had taught us to be careful.

One afternoon we sat beneath a straggly mimosa tree near part of the river that was called the Belly of Stones. Some boys were shouting and playing nearby. Below us the river swept past, dashing and throwing itself from rocky ledge to rocky ledge between islands of strange, water-worn shapes.

I narrowed my eyes against the glare. The boys had thrown off their wraps and were shooting the rapids, sitting astride pieces of wood and clinging on in the foaming torrent—sometimes tossed up high and sometimes disappearing as the waves dashed them wildly along. One boy came down a slope of water on his stomach, his arms fighting the water like the spokes of a chariot wheel. The boys finally clambered out and flung themselves down near us, burying their bodies in the warm sand, giggling and squirming until the sand clung to them like the skin of a snake.

I flung some flat pebbles across the water to see how far they would skip. But the water was too rough. I squinted through the sunlight at Tuthmosis. "How far south still?"

Anoukhet shrugged impatiently and disturbed two red dragonflies. They had been darting and flitting about with jerky movements and flashing wings as they tried to settle on her. "We have to have a plan."

"I *have* one," Tuthmosis said.

"What is it?"

He indicated with his thumb. "There've been Egyptian garrisons in all these forts. Even here at Semna and Kumma. But they're the last forts. Beyond here, we're in Kushite territory."

I had a feeling of dread. We'd traveled so far. Thebes was a dream from another life. "Who are the Kushites?"

"Southern Nubians," Anoukhet answered without looking up. One of the dragonflies had settled on her shoulder like a tattoo. I thought of Ta-Miu and her little cat tattoo and wondered if she'd escaped punishment.

Tuthmosis nodded. "Fierce warriors. Experts with bow and arrow and no fear of close combat and hand-to-hand struggle. They love nothing better than a skirmish. The land of Kush is rich in copper and gold and amethysts. My father wanted control over it but the Kushites fought hard. They refuse to fall under Thebes. They hate the Egyptians."

I glanced at him quickly. "That won't help *us*. They'll know Anoukhet is Nubian, but we're Egyptian."

"They hate Thebes. But when I explain how my throne was stolen from me, they'll back me. I'll have no difficulty in persuading the Kushites to act against Thebes."

Anoukhet squinted back at him. She was playing with a piece of grass—tickling a beetle as it crawled over flakes of rock and at the same time trying to prevent Kyky from snatching it. It was a shiny creature with glassy wings and a silver green body spotted with bronze. So beautiful, it could have been worn as a brooch. "Ha! They might act against Thebes, but why should they help restore you as ruler of Egypt? And what if they don't believe you're the son of King Amenhotep?"

"I'll have to prove who I am. They want a fair ruler as their neighbor. Not someone like my father who threatened to take their gold, their lands, and their women. I'll make a pact with them. An oath of promise."

I looked out over the river. Three men were trying to swim their camels across. The man in front held his camel's bridle rope in his mouth, urging him through the water while he swam alongside the grumbling beast. Behind the first camel, another man led two more tied head to tail. A man at the back did his best to keep them all moving in the same direction against the current.

That's what lay ahead for us. An impossible task. Trying to get the Kushites on our side would be like swimming against an even fiercer and riskier current. "Will your word stand?"

Tuthmosis scowled. "Of course! My word is the same as the word of Horus. I'm the god-king."

"Yes . . . but do the people in the land of Kush honor the same gods? They might not care about Egyptian gods."

Tuthmosis clicked his tongue. He seemed impatient—impatient that I would doubt him. "The gods don't belong to Egypt alone."

Anoukhet shot a look at him. "When will we leave to find the Kushite army?"

"Tomorrow."

I glanced back at him. "So soon?"

Anoukhet swatted the dragonfly from her shoulder. "We've waited too long. I'm ready for confrontation!"

Tuthmosis laughed. "You're always ready for confrontation, Anoukhet."

The boys had crept up on us. They'd discovered Kyky and wanted to play with her. A boy had found a chameleon on a piece of reed. He held out a dead fly and we watched the chameleon's long tongue strike out. On the reed the chameleon was the greenest of greens. On the boy's hand it turned a murky brown.

If we'd known then that the boys were spies, we might have behaved differently toward them.

The nights next to the river had turned bitterly cold. I was grateful to Kyky for snuggling between Anoukhet and me and warming my neck that night. The next morning, we stamped warmth back into our legs and began gathering our belongings. We thanked the donkey men for the time we'd spent with them. So as not to raise their suspicions, we told them that news of a sick relative meant we had to return to Syene.

We were preparing to leave when the boys from

the river came running to announce soldiers gathering just a short distance south in the desert.

"What sort of soldiers? Egyptian or Nubian?"

"Nubian."

"Are you sure?"

The oldest of the boys nodded. "My brother is a soldier with the Kushite army. I know these are Kushites. Their tunics have threads of red."

Tuthmosis smiled. "The time has come."

I took him by the arm. "Is this the only way?"

"You can't lose heart now, Kara. Not after all this time. This is what we've come for. To raise an army against Wosret!" He moved in closer and whispered, "Just remember, until we know we can trust these Kushites, behave like boys. Two women aren't safe with rough soldiers." He looked between us. "How good are you both with bow and arrow?"

I shook my head. "I've only ever used a throw-stick."

Anoukhet laughed as she slapped the dagger on her thigh. "Don't be scared for my part, Tuthmosis. I'm as accurate with a bow as I am with my dagger. I can manage any bow and arrow—or any man, for that matter!"

I saw her eyes flash and imagined she could. She had the height and the legs to draw a bow well—even a longbow.

We pulled on our boots, which were beginning to wear thin, and then gathered our meager belongings, making sure our daggers were in our belts. I felt for my girdle bag to check for the Senet board and my mother's bronze mirror. Then we bade our farewells to the donkey men, left the river behind, and trudged up the arid dunes ahead, with Tuthmosis in the lead.

He and Anoukhet seemed glad to be moving on. But I hung back, fearing the moment we would meet the Kushite army. Fear is not enough to describe what I should've been feeling.

We'd been walking for some time when we reached the crest of the highest rise. Tuthmosis and Anoukhet both stopped dead in their tracks ahead. I struggled to catch up. And then I almost choked at what I saw.

From the opposite rise right to the base of the valley and spread across as far as the eye could see in all directions were soldiers. Hundreds upon hundreds of them. An entire encampment. The noise of them rose up like locusts feeding their way through a field. Or swarms of angry, disturbed bees.

They stood with their dark oiled bodies gleaming, quivers and bows slung across their backs, sunlight sparking off their metal spearheads and shining against their polished leather shields, looking as if their weapons had just been forged in some fire mine. There were so many of them, so densely packed together, they appeared to be hammered out of one mighty metal sheet that spread itself over this dune and the next and the next. A vast shield of beaten armor.

I couldn't stop the sharp cry that escaped me. My voice echoed out over the dunes.

In one very still moment all went deathly quiet as if every man had heard me. Thousands of eyes turned to look at us.

21

MEN OF
THE BOW

I felt my legs give way. Tuthmosis gripped me
beneath my elbow and held me up.

"Be brave!" he whispered close to my ear.
"They're not enemies! They won't harm us! We
must find their commander."

I nodded to show I'd heard, but couldn't speak.

Some soldiers rushed toward us. I cringed and
squeezed my eyes shut as I imagined the sound of
arrows being drawn and the twang of bowstrings

being pulled. But everything was confused. I scarcely had time to draw breath and fill my lungs with air before we were surrounded and grabbed.

"Stop!" Tuthmosis shook himself free. "I can prove—" But he was hit across the jaw before he could say more.

Anoukhet raised her dagger and showed no sign of putting it aside. It skimmed the skin of a soldier's arm and left behind a bleeding gash. She lunged in all directions before it was knocked from her hand.

"Keep still! A plague of locusts on you, boy!" one soldier shouted as he grabbed her and thrust her hands behind her back.

We were trussed with ropes and led down the soft sand like donkeys or camels. Row upon row of bowmen crowded in on us, beating a slow, frightening tattoo against their shields and cursing into our faces as we passed. The heat and dust and raw smell of them terrified me. I could scarcely look up. The soldiers dragging us shouted at them to make way. The men slowly parted but not without jeering and pulling at our cloaks and shoving us along. I tripped and Anoukhet spit at one soldier and Kyky escaped from her cloak and went scampering off among them.

In a basin of arid dunes was an area barricaded with shields and staves to form an enclosure. We were shoved along through a horde of soldiers dressed in tunics woven with red thread and tied in such a way that long tasseled fringes hung down in the front. They had armbands of copper and gold and ivory and studs of gold in their ears— every embellishment worn, it seemed, to make them appear more fierce and their bodies more powerful.

We passed through a wooden gateway. Inside the enclosure was an area that seemed more like an entire town. There were shelters for stores and weapons and tented areas, and in the center, a number of raised platforms stood on thick posts cut from trees and were covered by large cloth canopies.

A man emerged from beneath one. His face twisted with annoyance. "Tie them up!" he shouted.

"If we're separated," Tuthmosis hissed as they jostled us along, "keep to the truth of our story. Remember what I said. I have ways of proving—"

He was given a sharp stamp across the back and his words ended in a groan.

"Keep quiet! The lot of you!" a soldier bellowed. "Take that one away. Keep him apart. He has too much to say!"

They led Tuthmosis away, and Anoukhet and I were each tied to a separate post.

"Hathor, protector of women," I begged, "goddess of the moon, right eye of Horus . . . protect me! Don't let them take Anoukhet away as well."

"Stop that!" Anoukhet hissed. "You'll only annoy them!"

I hadn't realized I'd spoken the words out loud. "Where have they taken Tuthmosis?"

She shrugged and then called out to a soldier. "Hey! You! We need water. And we need to speak to someone in authority!"

"You're prisoners. Prisoners can't make demands," the soldier sneered back at her.

"What have we done to be made prisoners?"

"It's said you were planning an attack."

"Three people were going to attack an army this size? Have you lost your senses?"

"It's what we've been told."

"Who told you?"

"Boys from the river at the Belly of Stones. They

spy on newcomers. They said you were whispering things."

"They're only boys! Not spies! How would they know anything? They were mistaken. We weren't planning anything. We work for the donkey men."

"Tell that to our leader."

"Take us to him, then. Or bring him here. Either way, I'll tell him."

"You're a cheeky one. You'd do well to keep your mouth shut."

"I'm Nubian and so are you. I'm asking you as a fellow Nubian."

"You might be Nubian. But the other two aren't. They're *Egyptian*, and Egypt is the enemy."

"All I ask is water. At least bring me that."

When the soldier brought her a gourd, she whispered something to him. He threw back his head and laughed. Then he looked over his shoulder at me in surprise and came across to offer me a drink. He went away laughing and shaking his head.

"What? What did you say, Anoukhet?"

"I said I was your slave."

"My slave? How could that be?"

"I told him you were a high-ranking prince in

disguise. That you bought me as your slave out of the kindness of your heart."

"Tuthmosis said we should tell the truth!"

"Tuthmosis isn't here. At least now we'll get some action. I said you'd reward them. I asked him to call his leader and to search for Kyky and my dagger as well."

"What . . . ?" a voice echoed above us through the slatted platform. "Am I to listen to a slave telling me what to do?"

"Not just an ordinary slave. He says his master is an Egyptian prince. He hinted of some exchange. He spoke of the great wealth of the prince. That perhaps something could be arranged."

"Which one is the prince and which the slave? They both look like ragged dogs."

The soldier came to the side of the platform and pointed below at us in turn. I looked up at the outline of the man above me but couldn't see the features of his face against the sunlight. He came down a wooden stairway and passed between us into the shadow of the platform, then stopped in front of Anoukhet and looked her directly in the face.

She dropped her eyes. "I'm not the prince, sir. He's there." She gestured to me.

The man turned to look at me. He was younger than I'd first imagined. He wore the same tunic as the others, armbands of gold, copper, and ivory, a belt of cowrie shells, and a short Nubian wig. His skin was dark and sunburned, but I could see he wasn't Nubian.

He narrowed his eyes as he looked at me. I stared back at him, but his face was still hidden from the light. For a moment he seemed startled. But perhaps I was seeing only shadows beneath the platform. He swirled around and commanded a soldier, "Cut them loose!"

"But—"

"Do as I say!" Then he sent the soldiers away and marched Anoukhet and me up the stairs ahead of him and wrenched the canopy aside. We entered a small, enclosed tented space hung with fighting instruments—bows, arrows, daggers, and finely honed axes and spears with such sharp-pointed blades that I shuddered at the thought of them piercing my body.

I turned to look at the man. Around his neck I saw a glint of blue glass. It was a common sort of amulet. Anyone could have bought a similar one in any marketplace. But then my heart skipped a beat. I saw the dreadful scar that marked his shoulder. Strapped to the stump of his right arm was a false limb made of wood.

"Can it be . . . ?" I whispered. I stepped toward him.

"Stand back!" he commanded.

His amulet . . . it was definitely a scorpion. "Katep . . . ? Can it be? Do you not know me?"

He took me by the shoulders and studied my face for a long time as if he wanted to be completely sure.

"*Isikara?* So it *is* you!"

KATEP

I stood staring at my brother in complete disbelief, my eyes taking in every detail of his weatherworn face. How had he come to be so far south?

He looked me up and down, but seemed more annoyed than delighted. "Isikara, what are you doing dressed like this? Why are you here? And who's this boy?"

I was surprised at the sound of his voice. But

then, for a moment I'd forgotten we were still in disguise.

I glanced across at Anoukhet. The sun was shining through a gap in the canopy. It struck her crop of gleaming dark curls. Her hair was beginning to grow again. She was lounging against a post, taking in the scene between Katep and me—her eyes not missing a thing. With her legs stretched out in that indifferent, confident manner of hers and with her short curls and cloak, she *did* seem like a boy. A very handsome boy at that.

Suddenly I could see why Katep was playing the protective brother.

He squared his body to face Anoukhet. "Don't just stand there. What are you to my sister?"

Anoukhet smiled across at him. "She's my friend."

"I can see that! But why have you taken up with her? What are your intentions?"

"Katep—," I tried to interrupt, but he held up his hand to stop me.

"My intention is to remain true to her all my life," Anoukhet replied with a half smile on her face. I could tell she was teasing him.

He glanced back at me.

I couldn't stop myself from laughing. "Katep . . . Anoukhet is a girl!"

"What?" He strode across and pulled her shoulders around toward the shaft of sunlight coming in through the canopy. It looked as if he might pull off her cloak.

"Stop! Trust me. She's a true friend. We've come through this together by being disguised as boys."

"But a girl! What will the commander say about having a girl in the camp?" Then he looked across at me. "*Two* girls, in fact. This is a camp of hardened soldiers. They behave like soldiers. They swear and curse and don't always bathe. They're a rough bunch."

Anoukhet smiled back at him. "I can swear and curse with the best of them."

"It's impossible. You can't remain here! What about the other boy? The one being held separately because he was causing trouble. Is *he* a girl, too? Am I to tell my commander there are *three* girls in the camp?"

In the relief of discovering Katep, I'd forgotten about Tuthmosis. I shook my head. "He's not a girl. He's the crown prince Tuthmosis of Egypt."

Katep shot a look at me. "*What?* You're traveling

with the crown prince Tuthmosis? It's rumored he was murdered. This is *truly* serious."

"Have you heard what happened in Thebes?"

He turned abruptly and stood at the railings with his back to us. "There've been many rumors."

I went across to him and touched his shoulder.

He spun around angrily. "Get back before anyone sees you! Is it true? Was Father poisoned? Was it Wosret's doing?"

"I'll tell you everything. But first, order your men to free Tuthmosis."

"They're not *my* men to order. I'm just the leader of a phalanx under the orders of a commander."

Anoukhet shrugged. "Speak to whomever you have to. But ask them to find my dagger and Kyky as well."

"Kyky?"

"My monkey."

Katep sighed. "Two women, a prince, *and* a monkey! What am I to say?"

He shouted to some soldiers below. Then he pointed for us to sit on some cushions on the floor.

"I thought you went to Sinai. Why are you here in Nubia?"

He shrugged. "The wind took me south. It's easier for a man with only one arm to sail rather than row. I kept going. When did you last see Father?"

"In Thebes. At Queen Tiy's embalming. He said he'd follow."

"He might still come."

"It's been too long."

"But he might. . . ."

"No, Katep. . . ."

Then I told the story and we interrupted each other in our hurry to hear what each was saying. Now and again Anoukhet added her own words. Every time she spoke, Katep looked at her with complete attention. I could see she held some fascination for him. When Tuthmosis was brought in, Katep gave him a curt bow and changed his attitude to become businesslike again. He turned to me. "Tell me about this Naqada."

I gave Anoukhet a sharp look. I wasn't brave enough to talk about Naqada.

"A scorpion," was all she replied.

A soldier came with Kyky and brought a message as well. Katep stood up and began pacing. "It's impossible! You can't stay! The commander will never allow it."

"Why not?"

"How can he allow Egyptians in his camp? Egypt is the enemy."

"He allowed *you!*"

"That's different. I'm a mercenary. I fight along-side whoever will pay me."

Tuthmosis nodded. "We will, too."

"You're not just *any* Egyptian. Your father, Amen-hotep, was his most vile enemy!"

"My father is dead. With the Nubians on my side, I can defeat the Egyptian army. When my throne is restored to me, the Nubians will be free of skirmish. They'll never have to fear another attack from Egypt. What is theirs will remain theirs. This I promise."

Katep shrugged. "He'll need some persuading. And if he agrees, you'll have to work like any sol-dier. Every person in this camp has a job to do." He gave Tuthmosis a sidelong glance. "And you'll have to obey commands."

I could see he found it hard to believe this person dressed in tatters, who smelled of donkeys and cam-els, was a royal person.

"The men won't stand for slackers. Even one who's the son of a pharaoh. Perhaps less so, when he's the son of a pharaoh! You'll need to earn their trust."

Katep sized Tuthmosis up. I saw him take in the scarred leg. Involuntarily he touched his own false limb. I saw Tuthmosis's eyes drawn to the wooden arm. He didn't comment, but Katep picked up the glance and a dark flash of annoyance crossed his face.

Katep would need to be won over. I didn't want them to dislike each other. "Tuthmosis would be of use to the Kushite army. He hunted with his father. They hunted lion."

"But he's never been a soldier," Katep challenged.

Tuthmosis shook his head. "No, I haven't, and you don't have to speak for me, Kara. It was my father who hunted lion, not me. I was just a charioteer."

"A charioteer?" I could tell Katep was impressed. "I'd give anything to have our army equipped with chariots."

Tuthmosis nodded. "Chariots give you the advantage of attack—right into the heart of battle."

Suddenly Katep was on the defense again. "Yes, but the Egyptians keep their charioteers as the elite of their army. Only the elite have special bows, while the rest of their foot soldiers carry ordinary bows. With us, *all* our men carry special bows. We are better bowmen."

I exchanged glances with Katep. He was testing Tuthmosis. I knew him so well. *Stop!* my eyes signaled.

His eyebrow curved up. *So?* he questioned back at me.

The thread that bound us like a spider's web was still intact.

Tuthmosis eyed him. "I'm a good marksman. Steady with a bow. But I've never killed a man."

I turned away quickly. I was afraid to hold Katep's glance because of the secret that lay among the three of us. Naqada. *I'd* killed a man!

Katep narrowed his eyes at Tuthmosis. "Are you a coward, then?"

"There's never been a need for me to kill a man. Have you?" Tuthmosis responded.

Katep shrugged. "I told you . . . I'm a mercenary. I work for the underdog. I kill where I have to."

These two were on warring sides. Fighting some strange hand-to-hand duel. "Stop. All this is of no importance. What are you doing here as leader of a Kushite phalanx, Katep?"

"It was because of my bow skills. The commander was swimming in the Great River one day. I was passing in my boat when a crocodile appeared from nowhere and lunged at him. It had him in its jaws when I shot it, using my false arm."

It was the first time he'd referred to his false arm piece. As if to break the tension, he nodded across at Anoukhet. "Isikara has no bow skills. What are yours?"

She tossed her head and laughed. "My skills? Ha! If I had my dagger, I'd show you. I'm as accurate with a bow as I am with a dagger. I'll manage as well as any man."

Her reply made Katep defensive. "It's not as easy as you think. We use the composite bow. It's strengthened with horn. You need power in your shoulders to bend it back."

Anoukhet needed no further challenge. "I'm strong enough!" She sprang forward and grabbed a bow from the wall where the fighting implements hung. She chose an arrow, fitted it to the string, then strode to the canopy opening. She pulled the gut back until the bow ends curved sharply and the feathers touched her breast as she took aim and released. It shot out over the heads of the soldiers and came to rest squarely in the wood of one of the upright posts of the enclosure.

In one stride Katep reached her. "Give me that!"

They stood with barely the space of a hand between their faces. He looked directly into her eyes. Then he gripped her wrist with his good hand and held it so hard that I could see her skin whiten around the edge of his fingers. "That's *my* bow. Don't *ever* touch it again."

I waited for Anoukhet to toss her head and spit out one of her taunts. But instead she looked down. And when Katep released her wrist, she turned and placed the bow carefully back on its hook.

I suspected Katep realized his victory. "I'll speak to my commander. It's up to him whether you stay or not." He looked directly at Anoukhet. "But you can't behave as you please." Then he turned to me and spoke as if I were his little sister stuck up in the fork of the mimosa tree. "And you can't suddenly become scared, Kara. In battle there's blood and people dying. It's dangerous and terrifying."

I threw my shoulders back and held my head high as I met his eye. "I'm prepared to fight. I'm not scared of blood!" As soon as the words flew from my mouth, I knew they weren't true. I *was* scared of blood. And I'd seen Naqada's blood on my hands. The horrible blackness of it in the moonlight. And I'd been terrified.

I thought of the moment when I'd crept up on him. Perhaps that's what being in the army was like. You had to forget everything. You had to kill like an animal hunting. It was kill . . . or be killed. A lynx wouldn't have worried about blood.

I'd done it for Anoukhet. Now I could do it for Tuthmosis. And for the revenge of my father. For the honor of his name.

Katep shook his head as if he'd read my thoughts. "The commander won't put women into battle. You need bow skills but only for your own protection. You won't go into battle. Your work will be in the kitchen, preparing meals and baking bread. Men can't fight on empty stomachs."

"What?" I looked back at him in disbelief. Then I tossed my head. "That might be so—but their stomachs won't be filled by *me*! I'm not going into the kitchen just because I'm a woman!"

"Soldiers take orders."

"You might be a phalanx leader but you're also my brother! And brothers are not always obeyed."

Katep narrowed his eyes. "Father was right."

"About what?"

"Right about you! You're stubborn and impossible!"

"So will you ask your commander if I can train alongside the men?"

"Yes . . . but . . ."

I lunged at him, trying to wrap my arms around him to give him a hug.

He pulled away roughly, his face reddening as he glanced at Anoukhet, who was smiling. "Stop behaving like my sister."

"I *am* your sister!"

"You'll train alongside the men, but whether you go into battle is another matter. The commander will decide. But first I need to persuade him to take the three of you on."

Anoukhet tossed her head. "I don't want to be treated differently. Why not remain silent? You don't have to reveal we're girls. Nor do you have to reveal Tuthmosis's identity. Let the commander think we're Nubian boys come to join the Kushite army!"

Katep shook his head. "Because you're not all three Nubian. The Kushites work on truth. The commander must know the truth from the start. He'll decide whether you stay or not. It's not just a question of the two of you being girls, it's a question of having a prince of Egypt—the *enemy*—among us."

Tuthmosis shook his head. "I'm not the enemy of Kush. The Kush and I have the *same* enemy— Egypt. I want my kingdom back and I'll fight to get it by any means. Even if I have to first defeat my own Egyptian army. The Egyptians are under the orders of the traitor, Wosret!"

"You'll have to prove you're the son of Amenhotep, the rightful crown prince."

My hands dropped to my side. Suddenly I was afraid. "He can't do that! If he proves he's the son of Amenhotep, your commander might decide to kill him. As you said—Egypt is the enemy."

Katep shook his head. "I give you my word. Tuthmosis needs first to prove his kingship. Then we'll persuade the commander that the high priests, by making his brother illegally king, have once more shown their greed and shown that the power of Egypt needs to be stopped. The commander doesn't want the land of Kush to come under Egypt's rule so Egypt can claim all her riches—her gold and copper and ivory and ebony. He wants war with Egypt. This will give him his excuse."

I turned to Tuthmosis. "How can you prove who you are? You carry no identity. Your cloak and broad collar were left on the other boy in the wabet chamber in Thebes."

Katep glanced at him. "Is there nothing?"

"I've this." He removed something from his girdle bag. "My royal pectoral. It has my insignia on it."

I glanced at him. Of course, this was what Ta-Miu had given to him at the palace. She'd handed him something as we were leaving.

Katep ran his fingers over the fine gold filigree with its lapis lazuli, turquoise, and carnelian inlays. Two falcons clutched Tuthmosis's name in a cartouche. The cartouche itself rested on the largest green emerald I'd ever seen. It was in the shape of a sacred scarab, the one who rolls the great sun across the sky. The heart amulet of a king.

"Perfect. Let's speak to the commander. Hang it around your neck so all will know who you are."

Anoukhet looked skeptical. "What's to stop the

commander from thinking it's been stolen? An emerald that size would be worth stealing. And dressed like this, he's more scruffy thief than prince."

"I have a tattoo on my upper thigh that shows the same insignia."

"The Kushites will use you as their pawn," Katep warned. "You'll have to convince them you can be trusted. They'll protect you, but only if you give them what they want—freedom from the yoke of Egypt."

When they were gone, I spun around to face Anoukhet. "So? What do you think?"

She raised her eyebrows and looked at me quizzically.

"What do you think of Katep?"

She turned away and marched up and down, pretending to inspect the bows and weapons.

"Well?"

"He's interesting," was her only reply. Then she turned around with a mischievous sparkle in her eye. "It's not just *us* who'll have to prove ourselves. *He'll* have to prove himself, too. Let's see what he's like in battle."

The sun had set over the desert by the time Katep and Tuthmosis returned. The soldiers were already lighting fires as the cool green light of evening crept up.

"What did he say?" I asked as they stepped through the opening of the canopy. "Can we stay?"

Katep shook his head. "Tuthmosis can, but not the two of you."

"What? Why should it be different?"

"Let me finish. Not until the men in my phalanx have decided about having two girls in camp. It's them who'll have to put up with you," he said as he withdrew from the canopy again.

Anoukhet's eyes flashed. "Ha! Put up with *us!*"

But I knew Katep was teasing her.

We tried to listen as best we could, but mostly we couldn't hear what was being said. At one time there was raucous laughter. I heard Katep say it was Anoukhet who had shot the arrow into the post. A single voice bellowed out, "She's a damn fine shot, then!" Then there were more shouts.

"But she's Nubian," Katep argued.

We could hear some arguing and a few "no no no"s, then some more boisterous laughter.

When he came back in, his face was serious.

"Well?"

"I told them you were useless with a bow and arrow, Kara."

I glared back at him. "Only a brother would be so brutally honest. Could you not say I was skilled with a throw-stick?"

"How would a throw-stick help in battle? You'd fell one man, then what? Your weapon would be gone!"

"So what was their answer?" Anoukhet demanded.

Katep couldn't keep a straight face any longer. He broke into a broad grin and burst out laughing. He handed Anoukhet her lost dagger. "There. It was decided on the strength of your bow shot and by the quality of your dagger that you *both* can stay."

I should have been cross with Katep. Instead I clasped him about the neck. He pulled my hands away. "Behave, Isikara. You're a soldier now."

23

FLETCHING

S o it was settled. We began training alongside the men, but all the time I was mindful of Katep's warning—Anoukhet and I probably wouldn't go into battle. We were learning skills for our own protection. I sensed it wasn't easy for Tuthmosis. He had to work hard to earn the soldiers' trust and friendship. It was eventually his strength and ability with a bow that won them over.

It was different for Anoukhet and me. Katep gave

up his canopied platform for us to sleep in. After dark we were left alone. But by daylight we were soldiers. And the men looked skeptical at the idea of two girls handling bows. They treated us as something of a novelty, like two exotic animals that belonged in a palace menagerie rather than an army camp. Strange creatures that couldn't quite be trusted to behave as expected. They gave us furtive looks and watched our every movement.

Each morning we assembled before the sun had risen with goose bumps on our arms. We stood shivering in rows while our phalanx was inspected by Katep. If a bow wasn't oiled to a gleam or properly strung with the right sinew, or an arrowhead was blunt, or a strap of a quiver worn or the grip of a shield frayed, we were punished alongside the rest of the men and made to do extra camp duties. It made no difference that we were girls.

We were expected to take part in everything— sword sparring against heavy bollards that hung from poles, javelin throwing until my arm felt as if it would fall off, and ax techniques that left me terrified and breathless. The only exercise we escaped was pulling heavy posts through the sand by thongs tied to the head, for strengthening the back muscles.

Katep took it upon himself to personally train us with the composite bow. He stood next to us hour after hour demonstrating the stance and the pull. He'd relearned his skills and pulled the bowstring with his left hand now. He used his wooden right limb with its pronged fork at the end to hold the curve of the bow.

There was much to remember.

"Relax, Kara. Bend your knees. Don't hold the bow arm straight out. Have it slightly bent at the elbow. Don't throttle the bow with your grip. When you draw back, keep an anchor point at your cheek, like a tooth that you touch with your bow fingers, so you can mark the place you pull back to."

He showed no brotherly favoritism. There were days when my body was so tired I almost begged to go on kitchen duty. But I realized it was for our own safety that he took so much trouble to reprimand me.

"Draw back harder, Isikara. Lay your body into the bow. Use your back muscles. A bowman's aim is to pull back so hard that the tips of the bow ends almost meet. You have to have power in your back and legs—like Anoukhet."

"Curse you, Anoukhet! It's easier for you with

your dancer's legs!" I hissed under my breath at her. Then I squinted against the glare and struggled yet again to pull back the taut sinew, until my back, shoulders, and arms ached with fatigue.

The bows were stiff and made of wood and polished ibex horn. They stood almost sixteen hands high. More than the height of a man.

Fine, for someone as tall and strong as Anoukhet. Impossible for me.

In the evenings, in the privacy of our canopy away from the men, I sprawled out on my mat and ranted. "I hate this! I'll never be a bowman!"

Anoukhet smiled. "Let me rub oil into your shoulders. It'll ease the pain."

"It's not just my shoulders. Every part of my body aches. And there are blisters on my hands. My thumb and middle finger are worn raw from pulling back the sinew."

It was Tuthmosis who showed me sympathy before Katep. He arrived one evening with two stone rings. "Wear them on your thumb and middle finger to take away the bite of the sinew."

Anoukhet's eyes sparkled. "How romantic! Stone rings instead of jeweled ones!"

Tuthmosis came to fetch me one evening. "I want to show you something."

He led me past the soldiers' fires to the far side of the camp where an old man was boiling two cauldrons of foul-smelling brew.

"Not supper, I hope?"

Tuthmosis smiled. "This is Kha. He's been making bows and arrows all his life. I've asked Katep if you can be his assistant."

I flashed a look at him. "*What?* So it *is* cooking you've set me up with, after all!"

The old man eyed me. "It's horn and bone I'm boiling, not *food*. Ibex horn is boiled to soften it for flexibility." He nodded at the other cauldron. "And those are hare bones boiling to make a sticky stew that will keep the layers of horn and wood together to make a strong and flexible bow. The jelly also keeps the cover bindings of bark and sinew in place so everything is held together tightly. The stickier the stew, the better it holds."

He sized me up. "Longbows are difficult to make, especially composite bows. You don't look strong enough! There's rumor in the camp. It's said you're a girl. But that matters not to me." He chuckled toothlessly.

"She's skillful with her hands. She'll be good at bow making."

The old man frowned at me from under his thick brows, then nodded. "Once you make a mistake—and you'll make plenty—you have to throw the bow away and start again. There's no sense in finishing a bow that's already scuppered. It's useless trying to right a bow that you know will never shoot properly. Bows need respect."

I looked from him to Tuthmosis. "I'm not sure . . ."

The old man sighed heavily. "All you need is a wood shaper, a sharp carving knife, strong fingers, and patience. Sit down." He indicated a place at his fire for both of us.

I moved so I was upwind of the steam and stench of the boiling cauldrons.

"Bow skills are based on how good your bow is. To learn how to be a good bowman, you need to be a good bow maker first. You need to make your *own* bow and arrows to understand bowing properly. None of these soldiers knows a thing about bow making. If I were their commander, I'd force them each to make their own. But I'm old and no one takes any notice."

He began to demonstrate with his gnarled, callused hands. "The horn of an ibex is split down the center into two halves. Then the outside is worked smooth and shaved down. By boiling the horn to soften it and then clamping it down, it stays flat once cooled. Then the horn piece is shaved into thin strips to fit the wooden bow piece. The strips are covered with hare-bone paste, clamped against the bow, and left to dry. The purpose is to make the bow flexible. To allow the archer to pull it back farther, without breaking the wood." He scowled at me. "Do you understand that?"

I nodded.

"A bowman is a musician."

"A musician?"

He nodded. "It's not about brute force."

Not about brute force? Katep should hear this!

The old man ran his fingers along a bow. "A bow-man must know what his bow can do. Know exactly how much tension it can take. His fingers must be as sensitive as a butterfly's antennae. Each shiver must be felt as keenly as a quiver in a lute string. When a bowstring is pulled, energy is stored in the bow limb. When the sinew is released, the energy is transferred to the feathered arrow. It's all very simple."

I nodded, even though I knew it wasn't so simple.

"Let me see your hands."

I held them out.

"Hmm . . . long, slender fingers, sensitive enough to be a musician's. But I see you have blisters!" He scowled again and shook his head. "I can't have you carving horn for bows when you already have blisters."

"What, then?"

He squinted back at me. "Are you good at bringing wildfowl down?"

Tuthmosis nodded. "She's superb with a throwstick."

"I'll tell you what, then. . . . You can search for arrow feathers for me. I'm getting too old and tired for bringing down wildfowl and plucking feathers to make arrows for the troops. You'll make a good fletcher."

"A fletcher? What's a fletcher?" I looked from Tuthmosis to the old man.

The old man sighed at my stupidity. "A fletcher is someone who makes arrows, as simple as that. He attaches feathers to the shaft of an arrow to give it lift. We need hundreds of arrows. In battle each man must have a full quota in his quiver. Without good arrows an archer is nothing."

Tuthmosis's eyes searched mine, waiting for my answer. I bit my lip, then nodded. Making arrows sounded like more fun than trying to pull a bow.

The old man eyed me. "So it's settled, then. Every day you'll report for duty and make your quota of arrows for the day. If the sun has set and you've not made the required number, you'll work into the night by firelight. There's no dragging your feet here."

So it was that Anoukhet became an archer spending most of her days training alongside Katep, and I became a fletcher.

From under the awning of the old man's workshop, sitting as far away from the stench of the boiling cauldrons as I could, I sometimes spotted Katep standing close to Anoukhet, guiding her shoulders and her arms, repositioning her head as she took aim. And sometimes, too, in the late afternoons when the sun had lost its sting, I caught sight of them walking out into the desert.

Each morning I rose before sunrise and went out with my throw-stick into the dunes in search of falcon and quail and guinea fowl. Sometimes I went as far as the river to bring down waterfowl. I carried them back to camp and plucked them well before handing them over to the cooks to add to the day's meal. The best feathers for fletching were the stiff tail and wing feathers. These I sorted and tied into bundles according to their patterns.

The arrows I made were unmistakable.

While I was out, I collected whatever wild herbs, grasses, bulbs, and fragrant leaves I could find for the cooks as well. I soon discovered from carrying them together with the wildfowl that some plant juices stained the feathers. It was possible to color them. From the crushed root of alkanet, I made red dye. From safflower thistles, I made orange. I boiled the dyes and steeped the feathers in the liquids. The light parts between the dark stripes and patterns took up the colors.

When the dyed feathers were dry and trimmed to shape, I slotted them into grooves I cut in the tail ends of fine straight saplings.

I was pleased with my work. So was the old bow maker. I could tell this when he held them up without comment and peered down their length to see if they were true.

They were fine arrows. Well made. Each with its own distinctive, unmistakable coloring. The archers were well pleased, too. Soon each phalanx asked for its own particular color and pattern combination. And each man branded his arrow shafts with his personal signet.

For Tuthmosis, I chose white feathers with no markings so the white took the dye entirely—wing and tail feathers of spoonbills, white egrets, and storks. But they were larger birds and more difficult to bring down. There was a beetle that if squeezed gave off a bluish paste. If Tuthmosis couldn't wear his blue Khepresh warrior crown in battle, he could at least have arrows of blue. Blue for eternity and life, to mark his royalty.

I made Katep's arrows with entirely red feathers. A dark, solid red. For bravery and fire. A symbol of life and victory. And I colored Anoukhet's arrow feathers green. Green as a symbol of friendship. Green because it's the color of happiness, energy, and power. To the tail ends of her arrows I added tiny shreds of red ribbon to tie up evil and as a sign of her bravery.

The old man, Kha, instructed me to make the arrows with small barbed stone flints instead of bronze.

"Flint is harder than bronze and won't bend if it strikes bone. Even if the wound is not immediately fatal, barbed flint heads are better. They have to be bound to the shaft in such a way that the head dislodges when someone tries to withdraw the shaft. With the head stuck in flesh or bone, the wound will fester and finally be fatal."

I shuddered. "It sounds barbaric!"

"All war is barbaric!"

I nodded. "War is not something a woman would easily dream up!"

Yet what about Hathor? Her double image was Sekhmet—the lioness of war, the fighting goddess. She was called on to vanquish enemies in battle. It was the lionesses of Sekhmet who lined the pathway to the Temple of Karnak—put there by Tuthmosis's father.

24

THE EGYPTIAN ARMY

The tips of my fingers became callused and strong with cutting and shaping the arrows. The days passed quickly as I searched for dyes and feathers and sat alongside the old man, Kha, listening to him tell stories of great battles and bravery.

When Katep called Tuthmosis, Anoukhet, and me to his tent unexpectedly one night, I felt my heart slip into my throat. I sensed something was about to change.

"Spies have told the commander that the Egyptian army has arrived. They are encamped a short distance away."

I glanced quickly at him. "With chariots?"

Katep nodded. "They traveled from the southern fortresses by boat and have dragged them the rest of the way through the desert. They're intent on war and forcing the boundaries of Egypt farther south. But this isn't their full intent."

"What is, then?"

"The southern boundary is an excuse. They've been sent by Wosret."

"How do you know?"

"Why else would they leave the forts and come so far south now?" He shook his head and turned to look at Tuthmosis. "Your brother's too young to be planning war. No. Word must've got out and traveled back to Thebes. Wosret must know you are here with the Kushite army."

I glanced across at Tuthmosis. This was what he wanted. But now that the time had come, I was terrified.

"Their camp is set up near some cliffs to the north alongside the river. Their chariots are lined up—too many to count. The commander has asked me to go under cover of darkness tonight to study its layout, so we can make plans for attack."

Tuthmosis eyed him. "I'll go with you."

"Me too!" Anoukhet said.

Katep shook his head. "It's too risky. Only you, Tuthmosis. You know the Egyptian strategy. How they'll use their chariots. Timing is essential. We need to strike within hours, while they're still resting from their long journey."

"Within hours? So soon?" Despite the weeks of preparation, suddenly I felt ill with fear.

Katep caught my eye and nodded. "We have to take them by surprise. Unprepared. Their chariots will be difficult to maneuver into position in the confined space between the river and cliffs."

The campfires were doused. Anoukhet and I sat hugging our knees to our chests in the darkness as Katep and Tuthmosis set out. They carried no torches, but in the moonlight we saw them creeping from the shadow of one dune to the next.

Suddenly Anoukhet jumped up. "I can't sit here waiting. I'm going after them."

"No! You heard what Katep said. It's too risky!"

"Are you coming or not? Make up your mind before we lose sight of them."

The soft sand muffled our footfalls as we ran. When we saw their dark shadows pause near the top of a sand dune crest ahead, we lay down on our stomachs and wriggled closer like snakes.

"What do you see?" Anoukhet whispered as we came up alongside them.

Katep's head whipped around. "I told you to stay."

"I'm not some pet dog to be trained!" Anoukhet hissed.

"Go back to camp."

"We're here now and besides—"

"Shh, then!" Katep put his hand across her mouth. "Just keep silent and do as I say. Keep back now." He edged forward on his elbows and peered over the crest. Then he beckoned Tuthmosis to do the same.

We crept closer as well.

An icy shiver went through me as I looked down.

A carpet of soldiers spread out from the base of the cliffs right down to the river. Their fires made as many stars as were in the sky. Their helmets, their spears and swords, and their linked armory on their bodies caught the moonlight and sent flashes of silver in every direction. And, as if to magnify their force, their armory reverberated with a sharp metallic clinking, more menacing than musical.

Behind them, right against the cliffs, row upon row of golden chariots turned silver in the moonlight. Even from where I lay, I could see the Double Crown of Egypt emblazoned on their sides. Next to them, powerful horses, like statues of molten silver, grazed from fodder bags lying on the sand.

Anoukhet wriggled alongside me and squeezed my hand.

Katep pinched some sand between his fingers and let it blow so he could tell the direction of the wind. He whispered to Tuthmosis. "It's in our favor. We'll be able to get up close without being heard. I need to be sure of their weapons." Then he turned to us. "Stay here. Don't *dare* follow! Use the call of the fiery-necked nightjar to warn us if necessary."

And with that they were gone, ghostly shadows sneaking down the dune alongside the cliffs.

"The fiery-necked nightjar?" I whispered into

Anoukhet's ear. I could hardly control the chattering of my teeth. "Do you know its call?"

In the moonlight I saw her smile and nod. "Good Horus . . . deliver us! Good Horus . . . deliver us!" she whispered back.

They seemed to be gone forever. We watched and waited while the fires burned down and the men began to settle for the night. The sand was cold. A chill wind had sprung up. I felt for the cowrie shell and moonstone eye at my throat and listened to the strange night sounds. The desert seemed more threatening in the moonlight.

We heard no call of a fiery-necked nightjar but from somewhere came the long, eerie shrieks of a desert hyena. I longed to be safely back at the camp.

Anoukhet wriggled her body to get more comfortable. "It's as cold as a dead man's heart. I wish I'd gone with them." She took a leather flask from her girdle bag, pulled the stopper, and took a gulp. "Have some!"

It was palm wine. I felt the warmth of it in my throat. I needed another sip to steady my nerves and bring back feeling into my arms and legs.

Eventually, when the moon disappeared behind

a cloud, there was a movement ahead. Two figures loomed up out of the shadows. For a moment my heart stopped. Then I saw it was Katep and Tuthmosis.

"What took you so long?" Anoukhet hissed.

"We had to wait for cloud cover. The moon was too bright to make a dash for it. Let's go! Hurry, now!"

When we were back in camp, the commander called a meeting with Katep and Tuthmosis and the other phalanx leaders. Anoukhet and I sat listening at a distance.

"So many you say. And their weapons?"

"The usual. Some fine-looking daggers. Bronze-headed spears. Plenty of khopesh swords with sickle blades, which don't seem too well honed. Looks more as if they'll use them as blunt chopping instruments. They'll break a neck easily. Or crush a windpipe with a good swing."

I swallowed hard. I didn't want to hear this.

Tuthmosis spoke hurriedly. "Their deadliest weapon is the chariot with an archer handpicking targets at top speed. The chariots are light and open-backed with just a handrail for balance and have the stronger six-spoke wheel. They're ideal for rough ground but will be difficult to maneuver in soft sand."

Katep nodded. "Their major mistake is that they've used the cliffs as a hiding place for the chariots, instead of encircling the camp with them for protection. If we attack, the chariots are deep behind their foot soldiers instead of out in front. They've yet to harness the horses. And there's not enough space to get them out quickly. Each chariot needs its own distance in order to allow for a wheel turn."

The commander looked between the two of them. "What do you propose?"

Katep smoothed a place in the sand, took up a stick, and began drawing. "If this is the river and here're the cliffs, we should gather hidden behind the cliffs, then come around on either side in a pincer movement, our bows at the ready. Without the chariots and the chariot runners being able to charge our lines, we'll quickly take the upper hand and control the battle. But the big element for success must be surprise."

The commander glanced around at them. "There's not a moment to waste, then. We must attack now!"

The meeting broke up. Katep went among the men of his phalanx and began to hiss out instructions and words of encouragement. "Keep your voices down! Make yourself ready! Our weapon is surprise! Strength to you!"

There was a brittle edge to his voice, but I knew this was the moment he had been waiting for.

I hurried across the camp to help Kha hand out arrows. Not all the soldiers were as brave as I'd imagined. Some came forward with their faces pale in the moonlight, and I heard quick incantations and from some sides even the sound of retching.

When Tuthmosis came for his arrows, I wanted to hold them back from him and plead with him not to go. But I forced myself to say the words he needed to hear. "This is your chance. Let Wosret know your strength! May the lioness Sekhmet fight at your side."

I could tell his head was already somewhere else. "Keep safe!" was all he said.

When Anoukhet came, she thrust Kyky into my arms. "Look after her."

"What? What are you doing?"

"Why else have I trained?"

"Wait for me, then." But she was gone before I got a reply. And by the time the arrows were all handed out, the camp was almost deserted.

"I can't stay, Kha. I have to join them. Look after Kyky for me."

"A battlefield is no place for a girl!"

"Anoukhet's gone. You've always said an archer's only as good as his bow and arrow. If you made the bow and I made the arrow, then surely . . . ?"

But there was nothing I was sure of.

He kissed my forehead. "Take care. Be sure to fetch this monkey from me afterward."

The troops were already far ahead. I could just make out the dark massed shadow of them crawling over the sand dune in the distance, their shields moving like the plates on a giant armadillo.

We had timed it well. Hathor was on our side. She had pulled her moon eye from the sky. It was that dark time that comes just before dawn.

The sand dragged heavily at my boots as I struggled to catch up. The burden of the bow and the quiver full of arrows weighed me down. I'd forgotten to bring a water skin and already my throat felt parched. I longed for a sip of palm wine now to still my thumping heart.

It was strange and unnerving being out in the desert on my own. A mist was sweeping up from the river. Wreaths of it hung low, hugging the dunes and lying in the valleys. I'd lost sight of the men, as they carried no torches. But from the stars that occasionally showed between the mist, I knew the direction to take. Once among the bowmen, I knew I'd find Anoukhet and Tuthmosis.

When I saw a figure approaching, I imagined it might be Anoukhet looking for me. But the figure was joined by others, and something about their outlines as they came forward through the mist made me change my mind. I began to run in the opposite direction.

"Halt!" I heard a rough Egyptian voice call out. "Hold up or we shoot."

I wrenched my bow from my shoulder and began to load an arrow. If I was fast enough, I could shoot before they had time to draw theirs. But before I had taken up my stance, I heard the unmistakable whisper of a feathered arrow in full flight. With no time to steady my hands, I pulled back the sinew with all my strength and let my arrow fly in return. The kick of the bow ripped me in the chest and knocked me flat to the ground.

But the kick was not from my bow. It was from their arrow. It had hit me just above my collarbone.

I felt around the shaft. My hands came away

sticky with blood. A wave of nausea swept over me. The arrow needed to come out quickly before the poison took effect. I clasped the shaft, willing my hands to stop trembling. Waiting for the rip and tear of flesh as I pulled, I clenched my jaw, thinking I would die from the pain.

But I felt nothing. The arrow had not been embedded. My moonstone amulet had blocked the full impact of its entry. The tip had lodged in my cloak and only grazed my skin.

But before I had time to feel relief, I was surrounded by three soldiers. They seemed more boys than men. One shoved his foot against my chest and pinned me to the ground. "Hold your swords, men! Before we kill the Kushite spy, let's find out what he knows."

My mind was racing. How could I save myself? How could I turn this to my advantage? I struggled to find the right words. "I'm *not* Kush. I'm Egyptian . . . like you."

"Not Kush, eh?" He bent down and jerked my chin toward the dawn light that was beginning to break and looked hard into my face. "You have Egyptian features, but you're too dark."

"I've been in the desert a long time. The sun has burned me."

"Ha! And what would an Egyptian be doing so far from Egypt here among the Kush?"

I bit my lip, trying to think of the right response. "You might well ask."

"So? Were you captured by the Kush? Or are you an Egyptian deserter? Which is it?"

"I . . ."

One of the soldiers grabbed me by the shoulder and wrenched me upright. In doing so, he ripped open my cloak. He stared down. "What? A girl! What's a girl doing in a soldier's uniform?" He pushed his pimply face close to mine. I smelled the fumes of wine and the stink of onions and goat meat on his breath.

I tried to duck away but his hand gripped my shoulder all the harder. He twisted one of my arms behind my back.

"I can explain." I tried to shrug him off. "Let go of me."

"No explanations are needed." He held a dagger against my throat. "Girl or not, you die! Scream all you want. There's no one to hear you!"

I reached back with my free hand, and with all the strength I had, I thrust my fingers at his pimply face. Thrust as hard as I could. A short, sharp jab that found the jelly of his eyes.

He sprang back in rage, clutching his face. "She's blinded me!"

One of his friends laughed. "She's not blinded you! But it would serve you right for behaving like a goat! This girl's got more to tell than you think. She carries a Kushite bow and Kushite arrows. An Egyptian carrying Kushite weapons will aid us. How far back is their army?"

I shook my head. "No!" I spit out. "You mistake me. I'm *not* a Kushite soldier. I'm a *spy*—a spy working on the Egyptian side, dressed to look like a Kushite to blend in with them. So I won't be recognized."

He shook his head. "The Egyptian army does not employ girls as spies. But *if* it's so, then you won't mind being taken back to the Egyptian camp to tell your story. If it's *not* so and you're a traitor . . . then how fortunate! Girls speak easily when under torture." He turned to the others. "Hold your daggers. We'll take her back to camp."

25

SEKHMET, LIONESS OF WAR

In the darkness I was dragged down the dune by the men and led into their camp among Egyptian soldiers sleeping on the ground. They grumbled and cursed at us for disturbing them. But before there was any chance of questioning me, shouts and bellows and more curses rang out from all directions.

"We're under attack!"

"Quick! Get the horses harnessed. Move the chariots out. Hurry to it!"

"It's the Kushites!"

I had no time to think.

Within moments soldiers were stumbling about, grabbing their weapons. Arrows were flying through the air, finding their mark all around us. Men were shouting commands. Others were clutching wounds. Horses were rearing and plunging, donkeys braying. Men harnessed what horses they could while charioteers cracked whips, grabbing their bowmen on the run and hoisting them up alongside them and at the same time trying to turn their carts.

Some men fell below the horse hooves and were trampled. Others lay facedown with arrows already in their backs.

In the pandemonium, I realized I'd lost my captors. I was loose in the crowd. I ducked low using the crush of struggling men as cover and scrambled to find my way among them. Trying to avoid the flaying hooves and trampling boots. Trying not to be dragged down or fall underfoot. At the same time struggling to keep under cover from the relentless hail of arrows that I knew, by their colors, were coming from Katep's men.

Hold up! Katep! Hold up! I prayed. *I'm here among them!*

But it was useless. How was he to know?

Suddenly I was wrenched by my arm and swept up onto the platform of a passing chariot. The charioteer clutched me to him and held me behind his shield. I turned to thank him, forgetting my Kushite tunic. I need not have bothered. He was the most evil-looking soldier I've ever seen, with wild eyes and the laugh of a maniac. The disarray of the battle had crazed him.

I wasn't being protected. I was being saved for something more important.

He let out a shriek of laughter. "You want a battle! *I'll* give you a battle! You think your men are good bowmen. Well, let's see how accurate your archers can be with *you* as their target!"

He flung me across the rail of the chariot and held me by my waist. My legs dangled freely in the air above the wildly spinning wheels and the horses rearing and plunging through the men. The soldier whooped and cheered as he wheeled around and at the same time took shelter behind me, using me as his human shield, while his archer took shots at the approaching mass of Kush bowmen.

A cacophony of howls, shrieks, and whinnying

horses rose up. The dawn was dark with arrows. The air around my ears whined with their passage. Then suddenly we galloped free from the throng of struggling Egyptian foot soldiers. The spittle of the horses flew back at me. The air rushed past my face. We were out in the open with nothing but an empty space between our chariot and the bowmen of Kush.

The charioteer ran full tilt toward them. I made out row upon row of them with arrows drawn, their shields strapped to their arms, marching toward us in a solid, unbroken mass.

I was going to die . . . killed by the arrows of my own men, arrows I had made myself. There was no saving me now.

In one dark cloud, a flight of arrows came straight at the chariot. I flailed and tried to wrench myself free, screaming out in blind panic, "Hold your arrows! It's me! The fletcher! Don't shoot!" But there was no getting away from the Egyptian's grip. In the noise of battle it was hopeless. No one heard me.

Hathor, protector of women, have mercy. Sekhmet, lioness of war, strike him down. Katep! Tuthmosis! Anoukhet—someone among the Kush, please recognize me.

As if in answer, in the midst of the noise, a shout rang out.

"Hold up!" It was Anoukhet's voice.

The rain of arrows from the Kushite bowmen stopped abruptly, as if choked by the unexpected shrillness of a woman's voice in the middle of battle.

A moment of utter silence followed.

The whistle of a single spinning arrow passed my face. I heard a thud behind me, followed instantly by a single intake of breath.

I turned. The arrow had taken the Egyptian high in the center of his chest. It had pierced his flesh and found his heart.

It was an arrow with green feathers and shreds of red ribbon.

His scream shook both sides into action. Arrows fell once more all around us. The wounded chariot driver clutched the rail, still holding me. I felt the warmth of his blood seep against my back. My own hands came away sticky with it as I struggled to pull free of him.

I caught the blurred movement of Anoukhet rushing forward. She leaped wildly past the horses and toward the chariot, trying to hold on to the railing and at the same time trying to wrestle me from the Egyptian's grip.

We were suddenly surrounded by Kushite bowmen. I heard the metal slurring of swords being drawn.

But before we could leap from the cart into the safety and protection of the Kushite men, the Egyptian archer grabbed the reins from the slumped charioteer. He wheeled the horses around so fast that the nearest Kushite swordsmen fell under the rearing hooves. Then he galloped at full speed back toward the Egyptian side.

Anoukhet grabbed my arm. "Quick! Jump!" she commanded. "Jump! This is our only chance!"

But my legs went numb. The spinning spokes of the wheels and the thundering hooves turned my knees to water.

In a blur of movement the chariot gained the other side and the Egyptian army closed ranks around us.

We were dragged off and passed as roughly over the soldiers' heads and with as little care as bags of durum wheat being tossed from the hold of a ship. Finally a space was made and we were flung down onto the ground.

Our hands were wrenched behind us, and although we struggled and fought and bit at our captors, we were dragged before a stake, pushed to the ground, and tied back to back on either side of it, our arms pinned and trussed tightly against our bodies.

"Be brave," Anoukhet whispered as she tried to reach backward for my hand. I held her fingers in my own as firmly as I could manage. "Katep and Tuthmosis will come for us. They know we're here. Listen. That's why they've let up their arrows."

Amid the commotion and confusion of horses and men and chariots around us, I listened and knew she was right. The hail of arrows had stopped. But for how long? The Kushites wouldn't care about Anoukhet and me. They were hardened soldiers. They wouldn't stop their battle against the Egyptians just for the likes of us.

"Vixens!" an Egyptian soldier hissed at us. "We show no more mercy to female soldiers than we do to men!" He drew his khopesh from his girdle.

Anoukhet spit into the sand at his feet. I cringed as I imagined a dull blow to her neck.

Another soldier stepped forward. "Wait!"

I could see by his cloak and gold broad collar that

he was a man of rank. He nodded his broad, brut-ish face in our direction. "They're bargaining tools. Not to be killed outright, but punished, rather! To use as an example. So the Kushites will appreciate the strength of the Egyptian army. And know we can't be trifled with."

He came closer and glared down at Anoukhet. "It was *your* arrow that killed our best charioteer? You found his heart!" Then he turned to a soldier at his side. "Cut off her bow fingers—so she'll no longer know the accuracy of her draw. Take them off well. Make sure the dagger is sharp."

I felt all blood drain from me. "No!" I gasped.

Two men grabbed hold of Anoukhet's right hand, spread her fingers wide against the ground, and pinned them down. I twisted my head from side to side looking for a glimpse of Katep or Tuth-mosis.

"Take her bow fingers! Take her bow fingers!"

"No! Don't!" I shouted as I twisted and tried to pull free. "Take mine . . . not hers!"

The man with the gold collar sneered down at me. "Why should I?"

"She's not a bowman. Examine her hands. She

has no calluses. She's *hopeless* with a bow. Her bow fingers are of no consequence."

"If that's the case, she won't mind losing them. But you lie. I know differently. She shot my charioteer. She was carrying a bow when she was caught. A very fine bow at that. With very fine arrows. So she *is* a bowman."

"By the truth of the feather of Maat, how can you be sure it was her? There were Kushite bowmen everywhere."

"What? You have the audacity to swear by Egyptian gods?"

"The gods do not belong to Egypt!"

Anoukhet struggled next to me. "Shh! Kara!"

"You're *Egyptian*—yet a *traitor* to all that is Egyptian," the man hissed. He turned to a soldier. "Take hers as well!" Then he kicked at me with his foot. "Be glad your punishment is mild! When the Egyptian army under the great Amenhotep last fought the Kushites, we took seven hundred and forty prisoners. From the fallen, we cut not just fingers, but took three hundred and twenty hands as punishment."

"What?" I spit at him. "Only three hundred and

twenty hands! And still the land of Kush didn't fall under Egypt's control. How pale a victory!"

He turned abruptly to the soldier. "Yes, by the gods . . . take her fingers as well. Teach them *both* a lesson. Take their bow fingers, now! I *command* it!"

A murmur went up. "Yes! Yes!"

"Take the bow fingers!"

"The loss of two fingers is nothing to me!" I spit out. "I could easily learn to draw a bow with my left hand." I stared at them unflinchingly. My blood was pulsing hot and angry now. If I had not been tied up, I'd have attacked them with my fists. "Take all my fingers! Take my *hands*, for all I care! That's if you have the stomach for maiming girls— you *cowards*!"

"No! No!" Anoukhet begged. "Don't taunt them, Kara! They'll do it! I know the campaign they speak of."

But before she could say more, the soldiers bent forward and spread her fingers again. I felt my throat constrict. Felt the words shrivel on my tongue. Then everything turned soundless. As if my ears were blocked. Yet I knew there was noise all around me.

The dagger came down swiftly. I squeezed my

eyes shut so as not to witness it find its mark—but not fast enough to stop me from seeing the spray of Anoukhet's blood that fanned out across the sand.

And then, they took the first two fingers of my own right hand as well.

26

TUTHMOSIS

Afterward it seemed a blur. What actions came in which order is hard to sort out in my mind. My head was dizzy with what had happened. So dizzy I thought I'd faint.

I remember the blind, numbing pain and my body shaking. I remember the vague outline of the man in the gold broad collar standing over us as we sat trussed together against the post.

Coward! I wanted to shout—to be so set on maiming two girls. *It's a victory for* us *that you need to cut off our bow fingers! It's a victory for* us *that you have sunk so low! We've more bravery in the fingers you've sliced off than you have in your* whole body!

But the pain was too great. My mouth couldn't seem to form all the words. Whether I spoke them aloud or not, I can't be sure.

A sudden swell of voices roused me.

"Victory is Egypt's!"

"The Kushites have ceased their fight! They've given up!"

Cheers broke out. Men beat their swords against their shields. The earth shook with the stamp of hundreds of feet. "Vic . . . tory! Vic . . . tory! Vic . . . tory!" came the chant.

"Given up? They *can't* have!" I twisted around to look at Anoukhet. "This is all *my* doing. It's because I was captured. They've lost the battle because of me!"

"Never!" she growled back at me. "They would *never* give up!"

A soldier pointed at us. "What about them?"

"Let's load them onto a chariot and display them to the Kushites to show how easily a battle is won when women are made soldiers."

"The battle is *not* over!" Anoukhet bellowed. "The Kushites would *never* cease to fight!" I felt her struggling to free herself. "Cut these ropes. I'll tell them what cowards the Egyptian soldiers are. That you hide behind chariots and horses using girls as your shields, while they, the Kushites, fight out in the open, shoulder to shoulder as one man. Free me so I can return to battle. I will use my *other* arm!"

There was raucous laughter. "She's a wildcat!"

The captain walked across and crouched down next to her. I strained my neck to see. He cupped a hand under her jaw and lifted her head so that she was incapable of looking anywhere but directly back at him. A horrible sneer was etched across his brutish face. "And then? What then, my lovely?"

"You'll be the *first* to die by my arrow!" Anoukhet spit out.

"I think not!" he sneered. "Do you think I'm troubled by the threat of a *slave* girl? We'll capture you again. And then it won't be just your bow fingers we'll cut off. We'll chop you up bit by bit. And your bowmen will be ridden down like dogs under our horses' hooves." He flung her jaw away from him and stood up abruptly. "*Then* let's see your Kushites come groveling and begging us for mercy."

"*Never!*"

"Don't you see they've deserted you? Don't you see what cowardly dogs they've proved to be for having retreated, leaving two girls to our mercy?"

"*Mercy?* Ha! When did an Egyptian soldier *ever* show mercy? Is cutting off a finger mercy?"

Without warning, an arrow whistled through the air and flew down at an angle, pinning the toe of the captain's left boot to the ground. Then another came in quick succession and shivered to a halt in the toe of his other boot. The arrows had bright red feathers without a pattern.

Despite the pain, I felt a smile creep across my face at the sight of the captain pinned down with two red-feathered arrows sticking up from his toes.

I twisted around to see from which direction the arrows had come, searching for a sign of Katep.

Then his voice bellowed down from the cliffs. "The Kushites have retreated by my commander's orders. But not for long. Look to the top of this cliff. You'll see five hundred arrows pointed directly at you and your men—each one marking the heart of his individual target. The commander has only to shout the command and they'll be released. Each arrow will find an Egyptian heart."

The captain's eyes flashed with anger as he searched the cliffs for Katep. Then he wrenched his feet free of the two arrows. "Ha! From such an angle and from so far, you'll not find your target," he bellowed. "You've not even found my foot!"

"I could find the mole on your cheek. We are the People of the Bow, remember. There are no better marksmen on earth."

"Be brave enough to show yourself, then."

There was a movement to my side. I saw an Egyptian soldier very slowly and stealthily lift his bow.

"Show yourself!" the captain taunted again.

"No! Katep! *Don't!*" I bellowed.

A dagger was suddenly at my throat, pressing hard up against my skin with its sharp tip. "You're better off silent!" the captain hissed next to my ear.

From the corner of my eye I saw a figure suddenly appear on the cliffs. It wasn't Katep but Tuthmosis.

"Let her go!" his voice rang out.

He stood above us totally transformed. He'd found a leopard cloak. It hung from his shoulder and wrapped his body with its great claws. Even from a distance I could see the gold pectoral shining against his chest. And on his head he wore the single tall white ostrich plume of Truth. He carried no weapons.

"So you're Katep! What use are you without your bow?" the captain sneered.

"I'm not Katep. Let her go, I say!"

The captain gripped me harder. His arm was choking me. I felt a small trickle run down my neck. Sweat or blood—I wasn't sure.

"Who are you to order a captain of the Egyptian army? You have no authority over me!"

"Do as I say!"

"What is she to you? What will you do to save her life?" he sneered.

I felt the blood hammer behind my eyes as I struggled to breathe. One swipe and the dagger would slice through my throat. One sharp jerk of his arm and my neck would be broken. There was silence. Everyone focused on Tuthmosis and waited for his answer.

"I'm Tuthmosis, son of Amenhotep. By my authority as king, I order you to let her go."

"King?" The captain began to laugh as he released his grip.

I slumped back against the post.

"Do you hear that? This piece of dirt thinks he is the son of the great Amenhotep!" He looked around at the group of soldiers, then threw back his head and laughed even louder. "Come down and prove you are king!"

With the speed of the leopard he wore, Tuthmosis jumped from the ledge right at the captain. They sprawled to the ground. The captain was taken by surprise. So was everyone else. Before anyone had the chance to react, Tuthmosis had wrestled the dagger away from him. Then, with one stride and a quick upward thrust, he sliced through the rope that bound both Anoukhet and me and eased us to our feet.

I stood trembling, feeling I would vomit. Next to me Anoukhet was silent.

I heard the soft swish of bows being lifted. Whether it came from the Egyptians or the Kushites on the cliffs, I wasn't sure. My body stiffened.

Tuthmosis stepped in front of us. "You may draw your arrows, but the Kushites on these cliffs are quicker. It's true what Katep has said. You are surrounded.

Each and every one of you has an arrow aimed at your heart."

For a moment there was complete silence.

"You will regret this day!" the captain bellowed.

"I think not!" Tuthmosis held up the heavy gold pectoral that hung across his chest. The carnelian and lapis lazuli caught the rays of the rising sun and glinted. But it was the huge central stone of the scarab that seemed like a living green light of fire. It sparked and flashed in every direction, invoking the power of the gods.

"This is the pectoral insignia of my heritage. It bears my name." His voice echoed around the cliffs and must have been heard by even the farthest soldier. "By this I'm the king's son. Appointed by the gods to rule Egypt. I am the intermediary that stands between the gods and you—the people of Egypt. If you harm me, you harm the gods. Their wrath will come down on you, and your families, and Egypt, a hundredfold."

I sensed rather than saw the soldiers around me drop their bows. A soldier next to me clutched an amulet at his throat and another drew a wedjat eye in the sand with the tip of his boot.

"The god of chaos will come down on you. I will put the curse of—"

I heard the soldiers gasp and call out to prevent Tuthmosis from speaking the name of the god of chaos.

"Ha!" the captain spit out. "Don't listen to him. If it's true and he *is* Tuthmosis, then it's true what Wosret said! He hides here among the Kushites. A *traitor* turned against Egypt." He gave Tuthmosis a searing look. "*You're* not the king. Your brother has been appointed by the high priests of Thebes as king. *He* is the living god—not *you!* You have no power over us! The gods will not listen to you!"

"Kill him, Tuthmosis!" Anoukhet hissed. "He's insulted you! If you don't, I must." She pushed through the crowd and tried to pull the knife away from Tuthmosis.

"Be still, Anoukhet!" He gripped her hand tightly. "I don't need his blood on my hands. It's honor I want . . . not blood! There must be no more bloodshed."

Anoukhet tossed her head and thrust her shoulders back defiantly. "This is what we fought for," she cried.

For a moment the two of them stared at each other with blazing eyes. Then Tuthmosis turned. I saw him take in the scene of the bodies of the dead soldiers that lay around us. "No!" He shook his head. "Look around you. Is this what Egypt stands for? Bloody battle after bloody battle? Men slaughtered because of the need and avarice of a few? This was my father's way. To show his power, my father made people die for him. Did that make him a *good* king?"

"Your father was a brave man!" The captain spit the words out. "You're nothing but a coward! It's good the throne is not yours. It's good your brother rules. Let's hope he follows the example of your father."

"Kill him, Tuthmosis!" Anoukhet urged again.

Tuthmosis turned to the captain with slate-hard eyes. He shook his head. "I won't kill you. But take a warning back to Wosret."

"Ha! Wosret has no time for warnings. Least of all from *you!*"

"This is a warning he'll have to heed. Tell him the kingdom of Egypt belongs to my brother. But warn him that should he ever send his army south again to attack the Kushites and lay claim to their land and possessions, by this royal pectoral I will return to take my rightful throne."

"What?" Anoukhet grabbed his arm. "No . . . you can't do this! You can't give up so easily. You have to take back what is yours *now*! We fought for this. We came all this way for you to fight for your kingdom. Now it's *yours*! Kill this man. Be done with it. He's nothing but a poisonous viper. Stand up for yourself. Let them see you are Tuthmosis, king of all Egypt!"

From the corner of my eye I saw the quick movement the captain made. He grabbed a khopesh from a soldier. I saw it glint in the sunlight. Then he swung it back with all his might. The blade came slicing in an arc . . . seeking to silence Anoukhet once and for all . . . seeking out a mark against her neck.

But just as the blade swung down, the captain's feet staggered from beneath him. His arm flailed wide. The khopesh flew out of his hand. He fell prone at our feet.

Protruding from his chest was one of Katep's red arrows.

And then suddenly, as if this was a sign, a hail of arrows pelted down from the cliffs. They darkened the sky as thick as a swarm of locusts and found their marks around us.

"Quick!" Tuthmosis grabbed hold of Anoukhet and me and dragged us to the nearest chariot. "Leap on! Hurry! The Kushite bowmen have run out of patience. We can't stay them any longer. The battle has begun in earnest. Take up any weapon you find. We'll fight our way through the Egyptians."

He snatched up the reins and wheeled the horses around so that the sand spun up in our faces and the chariot plunged forward. Arrows flew in all directions.

"Hold on well!" he shouted as soldiers tried to pull us down. "And pray the wheels are made of strong wood and the axle and linchpins hold."

Then, as we broke free, he grinned back at us with his leopard cloak flying and its paws clawing the wind and laughed as he saw our faces. "And be *glad* this is not the first time I've driven a chariot!"

27

ON THE BANK OF THE GREAT RIVER IN THE LAND OF KUSH

The four of us sat on the bank of the river in silence. The noise of battle had long since ceased. Behind us the desert had turned to shimmering gold in the evening light. Anoukhet and I each had thick bandages around our hands. We'd drunk the herbal mixture the old man, Kha, had brewed for us before he stitched our wounds closed with a horn needle. And we'd used the bee-sting ointment made by him to reduce the swelling and pain, but still my hand throbbed.

Anoukhet squinted into the last rays of the sun. I could tell she was seething. She narrowed her eyes at Katep and Tuthmosis. "Are you *both* cowards? Why did you wait so long to kill the Egyptian captain, Katep, and why, Tuthmosis, have you given up your crown?"

Tuthmosis kept silent. Katep gave her a look. "I killed him in the end."

"Only as he was about to bring his khopesh down on me. Why not before? You had the chance to kill him but you shot at his feet instead. Why? He was worse than a horned viper. He didn't deserve the chance to live."

Katep shook his head. "When I pinned his feet, I wasn't giving *him* the chance to live. I was giving *you* and Kara the chance to live."

"How so?"

"I couldn't risk killing him while the two of you were tied up. His soldiers would've slaughtered you. To rescue you we'd have had to kill everyone simultaneously."

"So why didn't you? You said you had arrows aimed at all their hearts. Why didn't you carry out your threat and kill them all? Why did you wait?"

I saw Tuthmosis exchange glances with Katep. "I asked him not to."

Anoukhet sat forward sharply and stared at him. "*Why?* This was a battle! These were People of the Bow who had their arrows trained on the soldiers of the Egyptian army who'd come south to vanquish them and capture *you!* This was your chance, Tuthmosis, to defeat Egypt with the whole Kush army behind you. Your chance to show Wosret your power. But you didn't take it."

Tuthmosis scratched in the sand with the tip of a reed across the pathway of a shiny green metallic beetle.

"Why did you stop Katep from giving the command to kill them all?" She turned her blazing eyes on Katep. "And *why* did you listen to him?"

"Because Tuthmosis is the rightful king of Egypt."

Anoukhet snorted. "It seems he has given all that up. Besides—he's not *your* king! You're Kushite now. You don't have to take orders from him. Least of all from someone who doesn't stand up for his rights!"

Tuthmosis glanced up. "I didn't *order* him. I *asked* him not to shoot."

"But why?"

"For the same reason I gave up my throne."

"Ha!" Anoukhet jumped up and looked down at him through narrow eyes. "Why did you give up so easily? You let the Kushites down. You let us *all* down!" She stamped her foot in the sand as if she wanted to rid herself of the thought. "Why? For what reason?"

Katep reached out and tried to pull her down next to him. "You're such a fighter."

She snatched her arm away. "What's wrong with being a fighter?"

"There's nothing wrong with it. You fight to stay free and true to yourself. You're fiery and independent. It's what makes you strong! It's not always easy to stay true to yourself. I had to leave Thebes to stay true to myself."

Anoukhet looked back at him with furious eyes. "You haven't stayed true to yourself, Katep! You let Tuthmosis overrule you with his princely ideas that have no meaning or place on a battlefield!"

"That's unfair, Anoukhet!" I was ready to do

battle to defend both Katep and Tuthmosis. I stared from one to the other as Anoukhet glared back at us. Around us the afternoon was filled with the sharp cry of waterfowl and the discordant croak of frogs.

I sat back and sighed. It felt as if all the air had been punched from my lungs. "What's wrong with us? How can the four of us be fighting? We've come through a fierce battle and we're alive. The Kushites proved themselves. They stood up to the power of Egypt and beat them back. The Egyptians have scuttled back to their boats as hurriedly as cockroaches looking for cover. And we weren't killed. We could've been prisoners marching back to Thebes. But we aren't. We escaped. We should be celebrating, not fighting among ourselves!"

Anoukhet scowled across at me and then at Tuthmosis. "*No!* I *can't* celebrate! I need to know why Tuthmosis gave up his right to the throne."

Tuthmosis looked back at her. "Why did you and Kara sacrifice your bow fingers?"

"We had no choice!"

He shook his head. "In the *end* you had no choice. But in the beginning, why did you go into battle in the first place?"

"You already know the answer. We fought for you. We wanted justice done for you."

"I wanted justice as well. I know you suffered. Many people suffered and died in this battle, wanting justice done."

"Their deaths stand for *nothing* now! Why?"

"When I stood on the cliffs and looked down, I was sickened by what I saw. There were bodies lying everywhere. I realized that to be the pharaoh, I'd have to spend the rest of my life in battle. Always plotting and vanquishing. The only way to fight fire *is* with fire. I'd have to send men to war, not because *they* wanted to do battle but because of *my* desire to stay in power. I'd have to plot and counterplot to keep ahead. To wrest and wrench my power from everyone around me like a hunter wringing all life from a waterfowl. As ruthless in my ways as my father and as Wosret."

Anoukhet narrowed her eyes but said nothing.

Tuthmosis broke a tiny piece from his reed and balanced it across the back of the beetle. "It's simple. Think of this beetle. If I pack too much on its back, it won't be able to move across the sand. When you're too greedy, you fail. Our quest was to grab back power. But not at such cost. I looked around me. I realized that to grab back power by violence is not a noble quest."

"It's what Egypt has *always* done!" Anoukhet snapped. "She's vanquished all the lands around her for their wealth."

"That doesn't make it right. You can't fight violence with more violence. That sort of power corrupts. I don't want to be an overlord recognized only for the power of my chariots and sword. Power is no good when it comes at the expense of others."

Anoukhet whipped around. "Ha! When did you decide *that*?"

"When I saw you and Kara have your fingers taken off. I vowed then. I held my pectoral in my hand and knew the heart scarab on it stood for nothing unless . . ."

"Unless what?"

He shrugged. "A stone heart is just that—a stone heart—whether it's of lapis lazuli or emerald. It's not the real heart. It's only a symbol, like any amulet placed in mummy wrappings to prevent the real heart from being stolen from the body."

There was silence as Anoukhet sized him up. Then her words came out like sparks spitting from a fire. "So you gave it all up! Our sacrifice was for nothing! We lost our bow fingers. You lost your kingdom." She snapped her thumb against the fingers of her left hand. "Just like that! All because you had a change of heart."

Katep pushed his hands down on her shoulders to calm her. She sat again. "You can't say the sacrifice was worthless. We each came to Nubia searching for something more."

"Like what?" she rasped.

"Freedom, perhaps?"

I looked around at their faces. Something nagged at me. I looked across at Katep and took a deep breath. "Can you find freedom when you've killed someone?"

Katep glanced at me without answering.

"I've killed a man."

I expected to see a startled look in his eyes. But instead he nodded. "I know. Anoukhet told me. You were protecting her. And she killed the charioteer to protect you. We've each killed for the love of one another."

Tuthmosis looked across at me. "Katep's right. It's behind you now." Then he laughed as if to break the tension. He picked up the beetle and held it toward me in the cup of his hand. "Here—I swear by my heart in the form of this living scarab, it's behind us."

I took the beetle. "Your heart?"

He shrugged. "Isn't a scarab more alive than a heart of any emerald?" He smiled broadly. "We've found our freedom. But if it hadn't been for you, I wouldn't have had the courage to be free now."

The beetle in my hand reminded me of the drawing on the Senet board. Suddenly everything fell into place. I jumped up. "Wait! I've just remembered something."

"What?" They looked at me strangely.

"I know the secret of the Senet board!" I fumbled in my girdle pouch and took out my father's board. "Don't you see? Look, there's a scarab beetle. Here's a frog . . . etched into the squares on the board."

Anoukhet clicked her tongue. "Scarabs and frogs are everywhere in Egypt and Nubia!"

"No, look again. Look at the other symbols. Think of the journey we've made." I glanced at Tuthmosis. "Remember in the labyrinth we found our way out because of the thirty turquoise tiles. We discovered the exit tile of Ra."

They were staring blankly at me.

"My father was right. It's a game of passage. Except we've gone the other way around. We've traveled in the opposite direction on the board."

Tuthmosis shook his head. "Opposite? What do you mean?"

"We weren't *exiting* at the Ra square. We were *starting* the journey. Entering our new life. Everything we've done since matches up with a marked tile on the board." I held it up. "There's the symbol of the net for the labyrinth and the wavy lines for the waters of chaos. Even you are here, Katep, in the boat." I shot a look at him. "See! Your outline is marked by stars. You're the hunter constellation, Sah."

Katep shook his head. "Senet is just a game!"

Anoukhet eyed me. "He's right. It *is* just a game. You told us the turquoise tiles in the passageway were unmarked."

I nodded. "They were unmarked because our journey was unknown. We didn't know what was ahead. We had to discover our journey."

Tuthmosis smiled. "You mean we had to devise our own game of Senet?"

"Exactly. Every square is a test, whether you move

backward or forward. The symbols are different for each of us. We pass through labyrinths, get sucked into the waters of chaos along the way, and call on the gods to rescue us. Everyone does the journey in his or her own way. The only thing that matters is that we make the journey."

Anoukhet looked across at me. "If we've made the journey, does that mean we've won?"

"I suppose it does."

"So now? What next?"

I shrugged. "To our freedom?"

Anoukhet jumped up and did a whirling dance around us in the light that was turning soft and milky over the river. "To freedom and new adventures!"

Katep caught her by the arm. "Will you stay here in the land of Kush?"

She stood still for a moment and seemed to dare him with her eyes. "Will you teach me to handle a bow and arrow with my left hand?"

"Yes!"

She tossed her head. "Then I will!"

"And you, Kara? Will you stay?" Katep was watching my face. His glance seemed to polish the thin silver thread that I knew still ran between us.

I shrugged. We all three turned to Tuthmosis. He shook his head. "I can't stay. I must go back to Thebes."

"Why?" Anoukhet demanded.

"To face Wosret properly."

"But you sent your warning. You said you'd given up."

"I need to face him—not with a sword but man to man. Justice needs to be done. I must defend my name. And the name of Kara's father."

Later the sun dropped. Katep and Tuthmosis went back to the camp to organize the dismantling of it. A full moon rose. It was a gigantic glowing moon that sent gold skittering across the river. In the glow that still lay in the west, a long skein of cloud turned turquoise. It floated low on the horizon like a fine transparent robe, touched at one end with orange cornelian.

I glanced at Anoukhet and saw she'd seen it, too. It was Hathor floating across the sky in her turquoise robe with the moon resting on her head and the last sunlight flaring on the cornelian of her cobra earrings.

I found myself smiling. I'd been so terrified of

those rearing cobras. But not anymore. They were our protectors. They'd spit venom on our enemies. And now Hathor had come to give Anoukhet and me her blessing. Hathor—eye of wisdom, truth, and secrets, protector of women, eye of the moon.

I felt for the warmth of my mother's moonstone at my throat and the cowrie shell as well. I saw Anoukhet do the same.

"You'll leave soon, won't you?"

I nodded. "I must. My father's honor must be restored. The Temple of Sobek waits for me."

Anoukhet raised an eyebrow. "The Temple of Sobek? Do crocodiles hold no fear for you?"

I picked up a flat pebble and held it awkwardly in my left hand, weighing it for size and smoothness as I thought about her question. Eventually the stone lay comfortable and calm in the cup of my hand. Then I held it between my finger and thumb, flicked back my wrist, and threw it as hard as I could across the water.

I held my breath, waiting for it to stutter and drop below the surface. But it jumped and skipped like a fish coming up for air—as good a throw as any I'd ever made with my right hand.

I shook my head. "Not anymore! None at all!"

Anoukhet smiled broadly. Then she searched for a flat stone and with a swift flick of her wrist sent it leaping after mine. "Every time Hathor carries the full moon between her horns, I'll throw a pebble and know you'll be doing the same. That way we'll never be parted."

The next day I bartered for two pairs of earrings in the marketplace. Nothing grand like cornelian or turquoise or gold—but simple agate, milky as the desert sand, carved crudely but well enough to show they were rearing cobras.

I'm wearing them now dangling next to my face. Anoukhet and I both wear them until one day we'll meet again.

Now I sit here on the bank of the Great River with only the last short distance to go before Tuthmosis and I reach Thebes. Only the lapping of the water through the reeds keeps me company while he goes in search of wildfowl.

On our journey back, I've written as fast as my hand will let me of all that has happened since that morning, alongside the river in Thebes, when the first transparent shaving of moon came into the sky like a fine, single thread of spun flax at the time of Queen Tiy's death. I hope my story will soon be carved in stone so the truth will be known to all. Poison, slavery, and murder are all a part of it.

Now all is told.

These are the words of Isikara—daughter of the embalmer at the temple of the crocodile god, Sobek.

May anyone who reads them know they are written by the white feather of Truth, under the protection of the Eye of the Moon.

AUTHOR'S NOTE

Two double-page spreads of three mutilated mummies splashed across a Sunday paper were the catalyst for this story. One of the mummies was believed to be the much-loved Queen Tiy, grandmother of Tutankhamen. Next to her lay a young boy with a severe leg injury, and next to him a mummy that was possibly Nefertiti, beautiful wife of Queen Tiy's second son, Amenhotep.

But why were the mummies sealed up in a tiny insignificant chamber, and why had their mouths been smashed and their hearts, the one organ needed in the afterlife, been removed?

Murder, mystery, and intrigue are part of the history of Egypt. This story draws on all these elements. Egyptology sleuths will soon discover I killed off Queen Tiy about ten years too early and allowed her son Tuthmosis to escape death. So that while the main historical events are accurate, a few liberties were taken and the city of Thebes has been called by its more commonly known name, rather than Waset, as it would have been then.

The fact that Egypt's magic is ever present was shown to me by some uncanny coincidences. I had presumed the crippled leg of Tuthmosis to be a birth defect but invented a chariot accident. Later I realized how close I'd come to the possible truth when in *The Search for Nefertiti*, Joann Fletcher observed, after examining the boy mummy: "I wondered if the family obsession with fast horses and chariot racing had had anything to do with the prince's horrific injury."

Another strange moment came with the original title I'd decided on—*Eye of Horus*. The right eye of Horus represents Osiris and the sun. The left eye represents Isis and the moon. They are the wedjat eyes and are always shown as dark. Yet when I went to print one, even though my black ink cartridge was full, for some mysterious reason the eye printed in the negative—white, pale, and slightly blue-flecked— exactly like a full moon.

I had found the perfect title—*Eye of the Moon*.

Don't miss the sequel,

EYE of the SUN

Prologue

✦ ✕ ✦ ✕ ✦ ✕ ✦ ✕ ✦

An owl swoops down. There's a strangled screech followed by an uneasy silence.

The sounds and rustlings of the night have set his imagination running. He feels that at any moment something will loom up out of the shadows. His skin prickles. His heart beats faster.

Who's there? he wants to call out. But there's nothing except the hoarse bark of a dog in the distance and the dry smell of dust in the air. Now a more pungent odor pinches his nose. Perhaps a desert fox is prowling for scraps of food at the offering altars.

He looks about uneasily.

The towering statue of his father glares down in the moonlight. His stony eyes are narrowed and unblinking. The edges of his gigantic nostrils flare. The carved line of his lips seems to sneer. Behind him the Temple of Amun is silent and secretive. Along its walls, carved creatures with curved claws, jagged snouts, and fierce fangs wait silently to pounce. And throats and chests of enemies are forever still as they wait for the arrows that are directed at their stone hearts.

All are frozen into silence by the bloodless moon.

The paving stones are still warm under his feet. His fingers feel for the comfort of the giant scarab beetle. The stone has been polished by the touch of many hands.

He feels exposed here next to the moon-splintered water of the Sacred Lake. This is the wrong place to have agreed to meet his brother. The inner sanctum would've been safer. In the inner sanctum the gods would surely protect the son of a king against the dark evils of the night.

It's strange to be back in Thebes. After the emptiness of the desert, with its far horizon and the wide stretches of river, his eyes aren't used to the boundaries set by the stone walls that anchor Thebes to the Great River.

And it's strange not to have returned to the palace.

No one knows he has returned. He has kept his identity secret. At all costs he has to speak to his brother first. He needs his brother's protection.

A sense of something behind him—an imperceptible movement—makes him turn.

He sees a face made pale by the moonlight. The hand clutches an object that glints.

In the moonlight the dagger is sharp and hard and unforgiving.

"*You!*" The word is more breath than sound.

The blade finds the soft spot just below his ribs and angles upward, seeking his heart. Two quick thrusts. Hard and brutal.

The blows make him gasp with their suddenness. No words are possible now. The blade is swiftly withdrawn.

He sees the hand that clutches the hilt. He knows it well. It's unmistakable. He looks down and sees the huge dark stain seeping through his tunic. He slams his fist against it. Presses harshly with both hands against his chest. As if in pushing he will stop his life from flowing from his body. But he knows it's too late.

He looks into the narrowed eyes of the face in front of him and sees the same answer in them. It's too late.

Someone calls his brother's name. Over and over. A voice that's surely not his own. It threads and weaves through the darkness.

Around him the night pants like a savage creature. The sky expands. The stars reel. His heart thrums in his head louder and louder . . . until he hears nothing but the sound exploding inside him.

1

THE ENCOUNTER

Thebes is the color of chalk—a mixture of sand swirling up from the desert and dust billowing down from the ancient limestone mountains. It sifts down over the city like fine bread flour. And this morning hordes of people with handcarts and donkeys pushing their way through the narrow streets were kicking up even more dust than usual.

I felt a shiver of excitement. This was going to be

the best market ever. Traders were coming from far-off Syria with exotic oils, woven cloths, spices, and nuggets of precious stone as large as duck eggs.

It didn't help that there was no ferryman waiting on the west bank of the Great River. The crowd was restless. Children squalled and mothers scolded. I pulled the rough cloak around my head and hoped no one would recognize me.

When a boat finally came, the crush was so great that an old woman fell from the quayside and disappeared under the water.

"She's not coming up! Quickly, do something!"

"Perhaps a crocodile's got her!"

"Oi! You! If a crocodile's got her, *you* won't be coming back either," someone shouted as a boy teetered on the edge of the ferry, ready to jump in after her.

He dived all the same and came up dragging the woman. They were hauled back onto the ferry. People laughed and teased as they picked off strands of waterweed from the old woman's hair and tunic.

All this took time. Eventually on the east bank, I was carried along by a surge of people like a bit of debris swept down by the flood. Men, women, large and small, old and young, all mingled with loud shrieks and yelps as carts were overturned, a child fell, and a dog was trodden underfoot. In the midst of this some geese escaped their cages and were honking and hissing and snapping at passing feet.

A pestilence of flies! My tunic hem was dragging in the dirt, and through some fresh donkey droppings as well.

There was a loud curse behind me. "Oi! Mind where you're going, stupid girl!"

I had barely time to save myself from falling under the wheels of a handcart piled high with onions and leeks, when someone held out a hand to steady me.

"Watch out! They'll flatten you as quickly as oxen trampling through barley," he shouted over the noise of the geese. "Come to the side of the road. You're limping."

I glanced at the boy as he examined my foot. He looked familiar.

"Your sandals are ridiculous with those upturned tips! No wonder you tripped! You need strong leather sandals on market day!" He pressed around my ankle.

"Ouch! That hurt!" I snapped at him.

"It's only twisted. But it needs to be bound."

I pulled away and tried to stand. "I'm fine, thank you!"

"You're not! Sit down. I'll bind it for you."

I looked back at him. Smooth, freshly shaved cheeks. No formal wig. His hair falling in damp tendrils against his neck. "Aren't you the boy who saved the old woman?"

He shrugged. "Saving old women or princesses, it's all the same to me!"

"Princesses?"

He raised a dark eyebrow and grinned at me. "Your rough cloak doesn't fool me. I can see by your fine linen tunic you're no country girl come to town on market day. You don't belong here, do you?"

I glanced quickly over my shoulder in case anyone had overheard.

"Don't look so dismayed. Your secret won't be told. It's safe with me."

"I'm . . ." I left off and brushed his hand from my foot, eager to get away. He jumped up just as abruptly and pulled me against his chest.

"Huh?" I gave him a sharp jab with my elbow. "What do you think you're doing? Let go of me!"

"I will, as soon as that donkey has passed. You almost got yourself knocked down again. Now sit calmly while I bandage your foot." He grinned at me.

"I know what I'm doing. This isn't the first time I've done this. Trust me."

He drew a dagger from his girdle, stuck its point into the linen of his tunic, and deftly tore a strip from the hem. Then he removed my sandal and began winding the strip firmly under my foot and around my ankle. I eyed him as he worked. His hands were quick and seemed practiced at bandaging. His forearms were crisscrossed with pale scars, and the fingers of his right hand looked as if they'd once been badly broken. He was about the age of my brother. About fifteen or sixteen.

He glanced up and caught my look.

I felt my face grow hot.

He smiled with perfect even teeth. "You're not from Thebes, are you?"

"How do you know?"

"The stupid upturned sandals. The braided style of your wig. Are you Syrian?"

I shook my head.

"Perhaps from Tyre, or Byblos, or even Kadesh. You're not Nubian."

I shook my head again.

"From where, then?"

"What's it to you? You ask too many questions."

He laughed, released my foot, and stood up quickly. "There. The way is clear now." He bowed slightly as if giving me permission to leave.

"Clear?" I turned to look at the people brushing past us, almost wishing another trail of donkeys could delay me. "I'm from Mitanni. The people here call it Naharin. But I prefer its real name."

"From Naharin?"

"*Mitanni.*"

He inclined his head and smiled. "So you *are* a princess! A princess sent from Mitanni to Thebes as a gift to the king."

"I'm *not* a princess!"

"But you *are* from the palace?"

I glanced sharply at him. "What makes you say that?"

"Why else are you wearing a peasant's wrap over a fine linen tunic? You've sneaked out and you don't want anyone to recognize you. But mysterious girls with cat tattoos are easy to recognize."

"Cat tattoos?" I snatched at my cloak. I'd forgotten the tattoo on my shoulder. A blush crept up my neck. This boy was a flirt. Yet even though I knew he was flirting, I was still charmed.

"I have to hurry," I said quickly.

"Go, then, Little Cat Girl."

"That's not my proper name."

He smiled and held my eyes. "Beware of carts and donkeys!"

And boys with dark, flirting eyes, I almost blurted out. But he turned before I could say anything and slipped into the crowd and disappeared.

My sandals were nowhere to be seen. Standing barefoot in the dust, I really did feel like a proper country girl. A pestilence of flies! I'd have to walk bare-foot through the muck, and my ankle would slow me down. The sun was stinging hot. And now I was late. And Kiya would be impatient for her length of cloth.

"Fine linen, woven with gold thread, with tasseled edges and a pattern of turquoise beads caught into it—is what I want, Ta-Miu," she'd said.

"How can you be sure I'll find such cloth?"

"The traders are from Syria. Everything at the market will be wonderful." She had sighed heavily. "I wish I could go with you."

"You can't, and that's that! It's too dangerous."

"I promise to behave. Please, Ta-Miu, let me go."

But all her flouncing and flopping about on her bed hadn't convinced me. I couldn't risk it. Kiya was too impulsive. She'd have drawn attention to us.

When she'd seen that nothing would make me change my mind, she'd pouted and said, "Bring wool cloth as well."

"Wool? This isn't the Khābūr Mountains, Kiya. We don't need wool here."

"It's not the wool I need but the comfort of it. I miss the feel of it beneath my fingers. Three years in Thebes haven't cured me of longing for things that remind me of home."

I had sighed. Sometimes Kiya—Princess Tadukhepa to others, but Kiya always to me— seemed such a child. How would she ever cope with her position as wife to the new king?

By the time I eventually reached the stalls, the market was seething with people. Over the stench of donkey droppings came aromas of sizzling goat meat and perfumed wafts of cinnamon, caraway, coriander, saffron, mint, thyme, and every other conceivable herb and spice. Hawks whirled overhead trying to snap up entrails, and were shooed off by angry stallholders. The hawks' screeches added confusion to the sound of foreign tongues, donkeys braying, voices arguing over goods, and volleys of slaps and curses as tempers flew and the day grew more and more stifling.

I kept a lookout for the boy. But in the mass of people pushing me this way and that, all I could do was edge my way forward and curse myself for not asking his name. He had come close to guessing mine. Little Cat Girl, he'd called me.

In a city as large as Thebes, I'd probably never lay eyes on him again. Who was to say he was even Theban? He might've been passing through for market day and be gone by tomorrow and on his way to another place.

I came to a stall piled high with woven fabric and trimmings, and I rifled through them. When I saw a cloth that I thought would make Kiya happy, I bargained as hard as I could and shrugged off others who tried to grasp it from me. Eventually a small sachet of ten orange carnelians tipped into the trader's hand did the trick. With the cloth firmly bundled under my arm, I shouldered my way through the crowds and came to a space where I could right my clothing and breathe freely again.

The cloth was woven with a pattern of fine red thread and was hung with tassels but had no beads of turquoise or gold. Not exactly what Kiya had asked for, but perhaps I could sew on some beads. I knew why she had to have something unusual and exotic for the banquet. This was the first proper gathering of all the royal wives since Nefertiti's marriage to Amenhotep the Younger. Kiya, being the youngest of all his foreign wives, wanted to make an impression.

Suddenly someone grabbed me around the waist and held a hand over my mouth. There was a whisper at my ear. "It's only me, Little Cat Girl!"

I spun around. "Are you following me?" I snapped.

"Only for your protection."

"Well, *don't*! I don't need your protection! I've traveled across the deserts of Syria on my own."

He smiled knowingly. "Not entirely on your own. You were accompanied by hordes of fierce horsemen as protectors."

I looked over my shoulder. "You think you know everything. Keep your voice down!" I urged.

"In this hubbub no one will hear us. Here. These

are yours." He held up my sandals with a smile that seemed to mock the upturned toe. "I found them alongside the road. The market is thirsty work. I know a place where we can get something to drink. Come."

He gripped my arm and guided me firmly down a tangle of narrow streets into a small alleyway. At the end of it I could see a glint of green as the river flowed by. An old man was sitting in a dark doorway. The boy handed him a bag of dates. In return the man poured out two horn cupfuls of pomegranate juice and pushed two honey cakes toward us.

The juice was bitter but cool. I was thirsty. The boy gulped his and was left with a pink mustache. It was difficult not to smile.

"I can't stay long," I said. "Tadukhepa is waiting."

"Tadukhepa?"

"Princess Tadukhepa . . . my mistress." I wiped the crumbs of honey cake from my lips. "Although she's three years younger than I."

"The *real* princess!" His eyes glinted in the shadowy light. "So I was right! You traveled from Mitanni with a princess. You *did* have fierce horsemen as your protectors. The finest and most valiant of horsemen. The Mitannians are famous for the way they train horses. Even the Hittites are jealous of them. And now you live at the palace here in Thebes."

"Are you asking or telling?"

"You don't have to be secretive. I can keep secrets."

"Perhaps another time. I must hurry now."

"Meet me again. Here tomorrow at the same time?"

Hmm. No "please" or "will you" from this boy. I shrugged. "Perhaps."

"Perhaps is good enough! Hurry, then, before you're missed. You've a banquet to attend."

I gave him a sharp glance. "How do you know?"

He smiled. "In Thebes it's not only dust that fills the air."

I took the less crowded route back to the river. Next to the new Southern Opet Temple a smell of myrrh drifted in the air. In the sunlight slanting through the columns, I caught sight of priests making offerings before the altars. They swung censers and mumbled incantations that echoed against the shining blocks of stone and newly carved papyrus-shaped columns.

Apart from the priests, there was no one. Not even the temple cleaning women, or the urchin boys who usually hung about pelting one another with pebbles and pestering people for a loaf of bread.

I hurried as quickly as my ankle would allow down the avenue of sphinxes that guarded the east and the west horizons between the Southern Opet Temple and the Temple of Amun. Along the way I stopped to touch the seventeenth lioness facing east. She was the one I always touched, the one with the strange expression that made her look wiser than the rest. Her body was warm under my hand, as if power were trapped in her stone lion muscles.

"So . . . what do you think about this boy?" I asked.

Her expression remained as wise as ever.

Then I hurried on down the long avenue. And as I passed through the shadows cast by the lions, with bands of sunlight between them, I felt I was zithering across the strings of a giant lyre. An inaudible vibration seemed to float upward. My feet were as light as air. My heart sang.

ABOUT THE AUTHOR

Dianne Hofmeyr grew up next to the sea on the southern tip of Africa. Her travels with notebook and camera to Egypt, Tunisia, and Senegal; through China and Vietnam; and across Siberia have led to stories that have won South Africa's M-Net Book Prize, the Sanlam Gold for Youth Literature, and the Young Africa Award, and have twice been named IBBY Honour Books. She is also the author of *Fish Notes and Star Songs* and several picture books based on Ancient Egyptian myths. Visit her at www.diannehofmeyr.com.

Goddess Girls

✴ READ ABOUT ALL
YOUR FAVORITE GODDESSES!